The Confessional Diaries of...
A GIRL IN TOWN

Intimate **COMPANY**

The Confessional Diaries of...
A GIRL IN TOWN

PAVILION

First published in the United Kingdom in 2007 by
Pavilion Books
10 Southcombe Street,
London, W14 0RA

An imprint of Anova Books Company Ltd

Design and layout © Pavilion, 2007
Text © Pavilion, 2007

The moral right of the author has been asserted.

All rights reserved. No part of this publication may be reproduced, stored in a retrieval system, or transmitted in any form or by any means electronic, mechanical, photocopying, recording or otherwise, without the prior written permission of the copyright owner.

Author: Sareeta Domingo
Commissioning Editor: Kate Oldfield
Editor: Kate Burkhalter
Designer: Lotte Oldfield

Cover image supplied by Corbis Images UK Ltd

ISBN 9781862057708

A CIP catalogue record for this book is available from the British Library.

2 4 6 8 10 9 7 5 3 1

Reproduction by Spectrum Colour Ltd, England
Printed and bound by MPG Books Ltd, Bodmin, Cornwall
www.anovabooks.com

CONTENTS

CHAPTER ONE 7

CHAPTER TWO 16

CHAPTER THREE 28

CHAPTER FOUR 46

CHAPTER FIVE 66

CHAPTER SIX 73

CHAPTER SEVEN 87

CHAPTER EIGHT 100

CHAPTER NINE 121

CHAPTER TEN 127

CHAPTER ONE

RELAXATION

Use your imagination. Use. Your. Imagination.

Each of you is possessed of the most powerful tool, the most powerful weapon available to us on this godforsaken planet – a creative mind. It is in charge. It is the master of all you survey. It can heal you, it can redeem you, it can transcend space and time, but it can also lead you astray. It can lead you to places you never expected to go, never wanted to go – at least, you didn't think you did. I need each of you to remember that. Nothing in this game of ours is impossible if you can focus your mind on what you want. On your desires. On your dreams. I know all of you have desires, or you wouldn't be here. You want to act. You want your lives to revolve around the notion of fantasy. And all I can do, all I am here to do as your supposed acting teacher, is guide you, guide your minds, towards those desires.

Now, that is the most positive thing you are going to hear from my lips. I think you're all crazy, but I was crazy once too, so I know how it feels. It's late, it's cold, it's a Friday night and I can damn sure think of about a hundred different positions I'd rather be in than standing here in front of you people. But fuck it; we're all here, so let's get this going. You're all tense as hell for a start, so it's lucky that's where we begin. Tension is cancer for the actor. You must seek it out and destroy it before you can do anything else. You need to take stock of every tiny inch of your bodies, work through every muscle and let everything go. So – let me take you on a guided tour . . .

MONDAY 13TH NOVEMBER
Relaxation exercise on bus home from work. Fifteen minutes. Started at tips of toes working way up to my head, paid special attention to the tension in the face, brow, etc., as instructed. Tension especially noticeable around the jaw, clenching teeth. Found it hard to keep tension from creeping back in, need to work on this.

WEDNESDAY 15TH NOVEMBER
Continued with relaxation exercises, around thirty mins today as I was at home. Began in seated position, straight-backed chair. Attempted to assume a position in which it might be possible to fall asleep, and began to explore the tensions within my body. Found it difficult to focus, but after a while I was able to work through the exercise and identify problem areas. Similar issues with tension in the jaw, etc.

THURSDAY 16TH NOVEMBER
OK. I've just looked at what I've written so far. You certainly make quite an impression, Mr Turner. Marcus. I'm not sure where to begin . . . but I don't think what I've written so far is what you wanted.

I've never really kept a diary. I can see why you asked us to do it – I mean, I think I can. It makes sense to keep a record of our work, of how we're progressing, I suppose, start to lay some foundations for later on when we begin to prepare for the play . . . Still. It's strange to think that you are going to read this. It's pretty late, I've had a fair amount of wine, and here I am in bed, scribbling away to my acting teacher in a notebook like some kind of old romantic heroine. I know I should probably have written more; it's class again tomorrow. It just felt a bit strange writing about practising my relaxation. Not that there's anything wrong with your techniques. If I'm honest, I have been thinking about you – your class – a lot. If that's any consolation . . . And I have been doing what you said with the relaxation exercise. I've been doing it loads, actually. I think I've needed it.

Everything's been a whirlwind since I moved to London; your class is really the only thing that's keeping me grounded. Ness (Vanessa from class – she's my flatmate) is in and out with a parade of reprobates, each one taller and more artsy than the next. Some of them kind of remind me of you, with the long unruly hair and dark aspect – except they've not got the distinguished greying at the temples . . . I'm smiling. This is silly. Anyway, Vanessa and I get on, and tonight more so with the wine – that she stole from work at the restaurant – flowing, but I can't say that her habit of absent-mindedly leaving the door open during sex has any calming effect. I don't mind though – it's nice to know someone is enjoying themselves. And I don't know, sometimes hearing them at it, lying in my bed across the hall, I start to enjoy myself too . . . Maybe she knows.

I'm a little bit lonely, I'll admit, but that's beside the point. It was my choice after all, leaving it all behind and heading out to the city. Leaving the shitty bank job, the small-town mentality. And you're right, people did think I was crazy to pursue my desires. I can still hear my mother amping up her Jamaican accent: 'Antonia Catherine Jenkins, what in God's name do you think you're doin', quitting your job? What you going to do in London? How you think you're going to make money prrrrancing about on some stage?' I can always tell she's angry when she doesn't call me Toni. And Dad's big green eyes, mirrors of mine, just staring at me in bewilderment.

Leaving was tough, though, of course. Leaving . . . people . . . behind. But he wasn't – they weren't – heading in the same direction as me. Then again, I seem to recall being reminded on a regular basis last week that we are actors, and therefore certifiable. I have to say, I am curious about you, about why you never attained the greatness you are guiding all of us delusional aspiring artists towards. I can't imagine it was because of a lack of ability, and your looks certainly wouldn't have held you back . . . Still, a bit of healthy cynicism is kind of appealing, and you wear it well.

So, should I be flattered that you asked to see what I've written here? I know you told all of us to keep a diary, but I have to say I was surprised when you pulled me aside as everyone was filing out. I've thought about that a lot, actually. But you have definitely cornered the market in inscrutability . . .

'Toni – hang on a sec.' I was surprised you even knew my name – I had the feeling you thought it was 'No', from all the 'NO, NO, start that again. What was that? Was that honest? No. Do it again.' It's fine, though, I can take it, that's what I've been after – someone to challenge me. It's probably too early to be lobbying for it, but I can't stop dreaming about what it might be like to play Angelique. The idea of an opportunity to audition for a new work by someone I respect as much as Brad Goldberg, someone barely a year or two older than I am who is really making his mark, was exciting enough, but since you handed it round on Friday night I've been reading his play non-stop, and that character immediately jumped out at me – so strong, so in touch with her femininity and sensuality, the power it can yield. Something in me identifies with her, and something in me also envies her. I desperately want the chance to put that across, to bring her to life on the stage . . .

But in the meantime I want to work, work hard, and get to a place where I feel ready, I have faith in my abilities and I'm proud of my achievements and the risks I have taken . . . and maybe to where you feel proud of me too, ready to let me explore those kinds of challenges. It just . . . it felt good when you said my name. I kind of got a rush of electricity when you said it. And then turning around and there you were standing behind me, the proximity made me jump. I hoped you didn't notice. Then again, here I am telling you, I guess.

But anyway . . . the purpose of this is for us to document our work. So I suppose I should do that. Properly. OK – relaxation. Like I said, I have been doing it a lot, sometimes more than the once a day you said. Every time I start, I can hear your voice taking us through the exercise. Telling us – telling me – to let go. Your voice in my head makes me so much more aware of myself, of my body, somehow. And something more, not just what you said, but a certain glimmer in your eye, seemed to be an unspoken instruction, not just to relax but to really release something – my inhibitions, my insecurities . . .

Now. I start with the tips of my toes. Lying on my back, I move them around under the sheets on my bed, and then I run the soles of my feet up and down along my mattress. The bedclothes are cool against my skin. I close my eyes. Reach my hands down towards my ankles, arching my back and pulling my knees up so I can reach them. My fingers creep slowly up my calves as my feet slip back down towards the end of the bed, and my legs edge down flat under the covers. I can hear your voice inside my head. That's it. Let go. I let the muscles in my thighs tighten for just a moment before I allow them to relax against the mattress springs. Let go. My hands have slid up towards the sides of my body, edging my T-shirt up, and my fingertips scuttle along, tickling my exposed skin, over my hips – as I roll them from side to side, my mind melts each muscle. My fingers play against my stomach, and my breath is getting faster – but not too fast. I can control it, like you said, like you are saying. Slowww . . . deeeep . . . breathsss . . .

My hands edge further and further up and begin to skirt the edge of my b— . . . but I slip them around to my lower back, and inch by inch I relax the muscles in between my ribs, will them to relax systematically, deliberately, up towards my shoulders – I let them sink in towards the pillow, and my fingers scrunch for a moment at the sheets before sinking down softly at my sides, and you are saying low and quietly – and there at the back of the neck – relaaax. It's almost as though I can feel you standing behind me, when I turned around as you said my name. Feel your breath right there at my neck, slow and warm behind my ear.

Let go. I stretch my neck back and push my chin towards the dark ceiling, air moving in and out of my lungs, slowww, deeeep. I move my head in slow motion from left to right, and open my mouth a fragment, my tongue pushing slowly around inside my cheeks and out over my lips, until every part of my body, every muscle, is humming with serene anticipation . . . I do this tonight. I've done it every night. And I know my body will remember the feeling; my mind will take me there when I need to relax, on the stage. Get into this calm space, my body – her body, Angelique's – ready for the journey ahead and the sensations to come. Your voice, inside my head, will melt me in an instant . . . Should I be writing this?

I can hear Vanessa downstairs letting somebody in. It's after midnight. I hear them creep with an exaggerated attempt at silence that has the opposite effect, down the hall towards me. I can see them through the crack in my door as I lie here, and as they disappear into her room I see the mystery guest peel off his T-shirt and drop it on the floor, his wiry back muscles flexing in anticipation. And the tension is back in my body. My hands creep up again over my hips, towards my stomach. Time to let go.

FRIDAY 17TH NOVEMBER
I just wanted to . . . I don't know, don't have time to write anything else but I don't know if I should let you

read this, what I wrote last night. Maybe it was a bad idea to agree to let you read the diary. But then again . . . I think you asked me to write this because perhaps this is what you want to read. Is it? I suppose I'm going to have to take the risk and find out.

CHAPTER TWO

SENSE MEMORY

Ah, OK, yes. Stop for a second. No, Toni – Vanessa. Hey, both of you, stop. Now, why don't I believe you? Have you ever had a drink in your lives? Well, it goes without saying, I guess, but Jesus! Is that what it feels like? Who here believed that? No. It's . . . you're starting all wrong, at the wrong jump-off point. What you need to learn to teach yourselves is to begin with the stimulus, what stimulates each of our senses in turn under these circumstances, and think 'how will that affect the outcome when we proceed under these circumstances?'. You need to recall the feeling through your senses, and they will lead you to an honest response. This is what will make what we see real.

I mean, you know . . . I'm having a shot of tequila – I can feel the tiny beads of salt against the tip of my tongue and I roll them along the roof of my mouth and swallow hard. I can hear the blood start to pump in my ears as I lift the cool, stout, solid glass between my fingertips and the acrid smell of the alcohol hits my nostrils, and I hold my breath for a second as I rest the glass against my lower lip and tip the burning liquid into my mouth, and I hear the 'clop' of the glass against the bar as my fingers feel for a slice of lemon, my teeth on edge before the flesh hits them and water rushes from the sides of my cheeks as I suck the acid fruit . . .

Feel. Every. Stage. You need to go through each stimulus and practise this until what we see is believable because what you are feeling is real; physically, sensually, emotionally. Real.

SATURDAY 18TH NOVEMBER

I felt like my face was burning through the entire class yesterday. It was difficult at first to tell how closely you had read this thing, the diary, what I had written . . . Your demeanour towards me didn't seem to change, but the way you made Ness and I get up during improv and show everyone how it isn't done felt strange – deliberate maybe.

Well, my arriving early was on purpose. I wanted you to have time to read it before we started. Somehow it seemed important to get it out of my hands and into yours. You glanced up at me, and I noticed that your eyes, seeming dark from a distance, were actually a deep shade of blue. I held my breath, and it felt like an age before a faint glimmer of recollection came across your face as I proffered the diary. 'Ah. Right. Good.' And you dropped it down on the seat of your chair as you turned to speak to the eager budding Jeremy Irons who tapped your shoulder. I retreated to a stray chair towards the back of the room, my eyes locked on to the back of your head as your fingers rummaged amongst the hairs at the nape of your neck . . . But as more people started to filter in I saw you pick up my diary, your back still to me, one arm dangling nonchalantly at your side as you scanned the pages.

Nessa blustered in and crumpled down beside me, a mess of shiny hair, bags, scarves and brightly coloured leggings, muttering incoherently to herself. She could see I was preoccupied, but as ever that was little deterrent to her launching into a tirade about how she thought last night's conquest had possibly stolen £20 from her purse on his way out that morning. I could barely concentrate on what she was saying, and I know it showed in my work in class too. For the first time in a long time, I feel like I don't quite know what I'm doing, and it feels dangerous . . . and freeing.

I'm not embarrassed about what's in here already, it's just . . . it's difficult to know exactly where it's heading, what I should be doing with this. Well. Except for that moment, you walking over before class started. I couldn't tell if you were making your way over to talk to me, or if it was just where you could stand and lean against the stage at the same time while you spoke to us. But you approached and just as you got to where I was sitting on the chair, you paused, leaned over and said, in that low voice, the same one that I hear in my head, you said . . .

'Yes.'

It sent a spark straight through me.

But . . . keeping the diary got me thinking. I've never really considered the notion of self-consciousness before. I was always the extrovert, the go-getter, but being here, and not really knowing anyone, and the class – it's all beginning to make me feel more self-aware than I ever have done in the past. It's unnerving – but I guess that's what I've been after all this time, some . . . stimulation.

Which is what I suppose should be the focus of this week's entries. What we did in class was useful, and I'm beginning to see how what I was used to as an 'actor' was really not what was required to get to the place I want to be in my career. Respected. Admired. And I can also see how, maybe, working through these exercises will help in my preparation of Angelique. Every day I am more determined to play her. To become her. To reach the place, the potential you seem – perhaps – to be pushing me towards.

MONDAY 20TH NOVEMBER
Vanessa crashed on the floor in my room last night. Derek, the guy from last week, was back, and apparently he is a terrible snorer. Still, it was nice to catch up with Nessa, like when I used to have sleep-overs when I was younger. We talked about the same thing that I did with my girlfriends when we were approaching our teens – boys. But of course now we had an additional dimension – sex. Having been in a

relationship for five years before I came here, I had almost forgotten what it's like to feel a new, different person next to you, the way they smell, taste – the differences in their approach to your body and yours to theirs, uncharted, mysterious. The way you are nervous and excited at the same time. The sense of anticipation, the eagerness to please. I've missed that.

Maybe that's part of the reason why Tim and I ended. Why I ended it. Don't get me wrong, sex was one of the areas in our lives that was always good, we had fun together, and being in love made the feeling of him inside me that much more special. After so long he knew every inch of my body and I knew his like the back of my hand. Just as I could tell by the tone of his voice what mood he was in, by a certain way he moaned I could tell how intense the feeling was as we made love. He knew exactly how to touch me, how just after we finished, he would pull out of me slowly and . . . and just as the tip of his penis left, he would cup his hand gently over me, the heel of his hand warm against my pubic bone, and rock it gently back and forth . . . it feels strange writing about this. About him. I forget sometimes, amongst all the hustle and bustle here, how much I miss him. Sometimes.

Vanessa's experiences seemed far more varied. She was no stranger to the one-night stand, and while on the one hand she told me how she envied what I'd had with Tim, on the other I could tell that she very much enjoyed sampling the fruit of many trees. I was impressed, however, with her fastidious attention to safety when it came to sex – the bathroom was always stocked with a rapidly dwindling but very regular supply of condoms!

Derek was, apparently, a lover of some distinction – not least because, according to Nessa, no one had ever gone down on her quite as expertly. It wasn't even going down so much as . . . bringing her up. She described a particular technique he had . . . Why do I feel like I can write this here? Well, you do keep talking about honesty, I guess . . .

She said – Vanessa – that his favourite trick was to let her climb on top of him, his head sunk deep into the pillows, arms resting nonchalantly either side of his body, watching her as she sat astride him, grinding her hips slowly around his hard-on, a half smile playing on his lips. She would writhe against him again and again until she could barely contain herself, and then, ever so slowly, she would begin to feel his fingertips creeping up, and starting to caress her bottom, still slowly, until they would be cupping each cheek, and feeding each grind of her against him with a stronger and stronger motion, until suddenly he would lift her off his cock altogether, and gently edge her, still bestride him, up over his chest, arrange her legs next to his shoulders, and lower her gradually down on to his tongue, which he would flick gently against her clit while she tried with all her might not to crumple in an ecstatic heap on to his face, the tension in her body only heightening the sensation as he began to suck softly on her clit until, just as she reached a shattering climax, he would grip her arse again and slip his tongue deep inside her . . .

I did let her know that I could attest to the fact that, judging by the noises emanating from her room, he did seem particularly talented! She told me it wasn't because she was trying to make me jealous, just that she thought maybe one day I might . . . Well, she made it clear that her door was always open. I'd say I was surprised – but with Nessa, nothing really surprises me.

In any case, having her in my room this morning and getting dressed in the dark once again reminded me of what I was missing. Having someone in the bed as you get up in the morning, feeling your way around in familiar surroundings somehow less familiar when there is a naked man, breathing slowly, lying nearby in the stillness. The unwelcome cool air against your still-bare back as you peel away the covers and his arms, the carpet soft against the soles of your feet. Rummaging through your cupboards and drawers, feeling for something familiar, every moment heightened by the sensation of his half-asleep eyes following your movements. That feeling of being watched and desired and walking away from 'last night', into 'today' . . . with just happy memories and no complications. I want that.

WEDNESDAY 22ND NOVEMBER

I've been thinking about what I should use for my sense memory exercise, and so far I'd been drawing a blank, but while I was on the tube home from work today, I was thinking back to those sleepovers I used to have when I was younger. The way we would analyse every experience, talk over every possible scenario. I began to think about how what seems so simple now was the most crucial, exciting, dangerous and sensual thing imaginable to our young, inexperienced minds. A look, a touch, and – were we to get so far – a kiss. These were our sources of awakening, the indicators of our burgeoning womanhood. And it struck me that there is so much sensation to being kissed. I mean really kissed. Not always necessarily the first kiss you have with someone, but the one that is like a mixture of feelings, that strong sense of desire, of delayed gratification, of intimacy.

Opposite me on the tube, clinging on to a pole distractedly, were a couple luxuriating in a kiss, a just-for-the-sake-of-kissing kiss, endless and dreamy. I couldn't look away. I was envious. But it also sparked something in me. I can't describe it but I could almost *feel* the sensation just by thinking of the feelings, the sensations involved – just like you said.

I found myself pondering what would be necessary, what sensations I would need to run through in my head to reach a place where I could convey that sensation of having been kissed so . . . so thoroughly, feeling so completely enraptured by it.

When I got home this evening, Nessa wasn't home – working the late shift at the restaurant – so I had the flat to myself. I settled into a chair and went through my relaxation exercise, like you taught us, but I was careful not to get too carried away with myself. Taking slow, deep breaths I worked through every part of my body until I was completely relaxed and ready to start. Like you told us, I took each of the five senses in turn. Asked myself every possible question I could about each of those five aspects, to create a full sensation of what that feeling is like, just using my mind. I was surprised at just how much my head was buzzing with anticipation at the idea of it.

Sight.

Looking up and . . . his dark eyes, eyes that seem dark at least until you get . . . His eyes are looking down at me, lashes thick and long, flicking down towards me, his head turned a fraction to the side, and I can see the muscles in his jaw flex and relax as he clenches his teeth, almost as though he is trying to stop himself from pouncing too soon. He doesn't lower his face towards me, he lets me study the angle of that defiant jaw-line a while, but the second his face begins to move towards mine, just a fraction closer, my eyelids swoop downwards and I am plunged into the velvet red darkness behind them, the more to heighten my other senses. And so I turn to –

Hearing.

With my eyes closed, my heartbeat seems amplified tenfold. I can hear my breath quickening at the mere thought of his lips touching mine, though that sweet moment has not yet arrived, but air ripples in and out between my lips until his face nears mine and I hear my sudden intake of breath, which then stops for a moment, then I hear it begin again in stuttering bursts through my nose, and I hear my feet shuffle, angling for a better position to steady myself as we get closer and closer to the moment I long for –

Smell.

As his body leans closer I can smell the earthy wool of his jumper . . . he wears it next to his skin, unshielded, and the warmth between us heightens his scent – clean, soapy, but mixed with something musky, masculine and unexplainably erotic – and mine, softer, more familiar until now as it mingles with his it becomes greater, a more sensual version of me. The smell of us together gets stronger and stronger, mixing, intertwining until almost without warning –

Touch.

His lips suddenly touch mine. Gently at first, and then he pulls away a fraction, just barely, our breath heating the space between our mouths. And then they are there again, against my lips, brushing each against my own slowly, until they tingle with electricity. Then growing in pressure, and I return that pressure, suddenly we are battling together but united, my lips and his, and I groan as his tongue sweeps slowly into and out of my mouth, and again, and my tongue into his. His feels dextrous and strong, and I can feel his stubble scratch against my face, a beautiful fire against my chin, and I reach my hands up against his face, my palm flat against his cheek and my fingertips play against the soft greying hair at his temple, his unkempt mane brushing against my forehead and I feel his hands slide up against my sides, his fingers find the join between my skirt and my T-shirt and play at my hips where they have exposed bare skin, and I am enraptured by his –

Taste.

It is both salty and sweet like some exotic fruit, so familiar and human, yet so foreign to my own mouth that my taste buds sing at the sensation of him, I drink him down, I cannot contain my ecstasy.

THURSDAY 23RD NOVEMBER
I feel as though I spend most of my time at work daydreaming about this – thinking about the sense-memory exercise. About that kiss. I must have been drifting off yesterday while Michelle blathered on

about going through our sections to check the core stock, because the random check made it clear that I had not been going through the books and weeding out the things I had put in on a whim (our 'Plays' section is full of Shakespeare and Alan Bennett – nothing to turn the heads of the more adventurous). Needless to say, Michelle didn't appreciate my additions. Still, working in the bookshop gives me downtime to practise my acting exercises in the back room when I'm on a break. It's beginning to get under my skin thinking about it. Fantasizing endlessly on each minute sensation caused by the kiss. I am convinced that I can almost feel it happening as I think through the exercise, to the point where perhaps . . . perhaps I don't even need that kiss to really happen. I don't know. Maybe me thinking it into existence, and you reading it . . . maybe that will be enough for now.

It's just that . . . it's almost as if, each time I do the exercise, that it is really happening. That I can really feel your lips against my lips, and your tongue inside my mouth, and your hands against my waist, and my fingertips playing in your hair.

And what surprises me the most is . . . What surprises me is that I am not scared now. Each time I go through the exercise I am more and more certain of my lack of fear in doing this. I am not scared of writing this and giving it to you. The question is – what will you think when you read it?

CHAPTER THREE

CONCENTRATION

Acting is like being in an insane asylum. And you people are the nutters. There you are, on the stage, pretending to be something that you are not, usually whilst standing on a raised platform of wood, in front of a group of people who you will pretend are not there. But what do you know? There we actors are, getting away with this kind of behaviour day in and day out. The trick, you see, is to convince them – the audience – that you are so enraptured, so involved in what you are doing on that stage that you truly do not know of their existence.

How do you do that? It's not complicated. You have to concentrate. You have to focus so wholly on something within that false reality you are portraying that you become completely unaware of being watched. When we hear that phrase 'being immersed in a role', that's what they're on about. You are underwater, oblivious yet visible to all.

So – what are you concentrating on? That is up to you. It can be a physical object. It can be a specific emotion or stimulus or you can just be conjugating French verbs in your head. It can be the other person in the scene. Anything. But you must concentrate. Or you may as well make your way to the nut house, because if you don't concentrate, you aren't convincing, and then the audience isn't gonna give a shit.

SATURDAY 25TH NOVEMBER

You asked me for it yesterday, before I could offer it to you. You asked me for my diary. I was avoiding you, trying not to make eye contact and deliberately arriving five minutes after class had started – just my luck that the District Line was down and half the class was later than me. And there you were, ambling over towards me in that detached, nonchalant manner of yours, chewing on the end of your pen, but with your eyes locked on me. I could feel them before I looked up. 'So.' That was all you said at first. But I knew what you meant. For all my bravado when I was writing, I suddenly felt a bit too honest. I hadn't really thought about what the consequences of what I had written might be, and all at once I felt a deep sense of vulnerability. You could mock me; you could be shocked, horrified, dismissive. Any number of things. But oddly that feeling only lasted a moment. The minute I opened my mouth something took over, a sense of defiance.

'So?'

And you smiled. I nearly died. Could you tell? I don't think I had ever seen you smile during class, and never once in my direction. It took all my strength not to beam at you and scrabble desperately in my bag looking for the diary. Even now . . . knowing you are going to be reading every word I write on this page, and those to come, it's as if I can't predict what your reaction will be, and so all I can do is put it out there for you to read. It's like the concentration exercise I guess – I have become unaware of you, my audience.

I'm laughing. I know that definitely isn't true. But I guess the delay, the lack of immediacy with writing this down, in comparison to what I feel on the stage, is what makes it easier in a way. On the other hand, especially now, knowing you are so close by, and your note, and . . . it makes it very hard not to allow you to be the thing on which I concentrate . . .

I was confused at first, when you said in class that you would give the diary back to me tomorrow, Saturday. Today. At first I thought it was some kind of veiled come-on that I was slightly too naïve to understand, but when you explained how you had seen me once or twice, getting off the bus up the road while you sat in your front room, I was somewhat mortified, I have to admit. The idea of you seeing me, harassed after work or coming back from a trip to the shops, frazzled and unkempt, was very worrying indeed. But then again. You saw me. You were watching me. It made me feel . . . safe. And excited. In fact, it was almost as though I detected a hint of apprehension as the words escaped your lips – 'I'll just pop it through your door on my way out on Saturday morning' . . . You could only be living a few minutes away from our block of flats. You knew which block was mine; you'd watched me go into it, perfectly unaware of my audience. You were watching me. But it feels somehow like a thousand different things have happened between then and now. Between you saying that and what happened yesterday, last night . . . and this morning.

Forming our pairs for the improvisations was amusing; Nessa almost had a fit when Jon walked over to me. She had been eyeing him in an uncharacteristically demure fashion since the course began, and there he was, slipping through her fingers. I have to say I wasn't as surprised as she might have been. I had felt him watching me a couple of times – either he was impressed with some of what I had done in class, or he was sizing me up in some other way. I couldn't be sure, but I felt his eyes.

I was just excited to start doing some focused work on the Goldberg play, even if it was ostensibly just an improv on concentration . . . on seduction. It still felt like I was getting closer to Angelique, to the state of mind I need to get to in order to play her, to become her. In a way it feels like every step I'm making is taking me closer to her. But it's also been difficult to shake off this self-awareness I've been kindling. When the class began to pair off and Jon came over to me, I felt a slight tingle of vulnerability, but at the same time something pulled me towards him, something familiar yet distant – an attraction I hadn't felt in a very long time. It feels strange writing that here.

Admitting that to you. But I think we are past the point of politeness now. And I can't help but feel that in some way you were trying to provoke something from me. I have this constant feeling that you are trying to orchestrate something, but I'm not sure what . . . All I do know is that my life is getting more interesting every day in this city, and that you, and the class, have a lot to do with it.

There was a sense of expectation as we all gathered around tentatively next to our newly chosen partners, with you mingling amongst us, prowling almost, with that sly sense of danger playing across your features. I knew almost before your index finger swept up from your side and pointed towards us that you would choose Jon and me. And I knew that you knew from the way your mouth curled up ever so slightly at the corner as you motioned us into the middle of the floor. You brushed close to me as we walked towards the centre of the group of students, and whispered, almost imperceptibly in my ear, 'Show him what you've got . . .'

Jon and I stood facing one another while you walked around us clearing a space, creating a circle of students watching us critically. I didn't quite know what you had in store for us but, whatever it was, I was eager to prove that I could rise to the challenge. A silence settled amongst the class. You moved away, outside of the group, and motioned for Jon to follow –

I could see you speaking in a low voice to him, giving him some instruction, while he nodded intently. Then, suddenly, you were behind me. It felt like every single person there – especially every woman – fixed their eyes upon us, as you whispered . . .

'Don't turn around. Listen. I want you to concentrate on one thing. No matter what happens, I want you to focus on the idea that you have to get this man inside you. You must use everything in your power to get him to fuck you. And I don't mean gentle, sweet lovemaking. You have to convince him that he hasn't lived until he's felt what it is like to make you wet.'

I was overwhelmed. I couldn't tell if anybody else could hear what you were saying; the way you spoke was so intimate, I could hardly breathe. Everything slowed down, and it felt as though I was sucking the energy from your body, the electricity that seared through my body from the top of my head right down to the centre of me, and then channelling it. It was as though something took over me, and the instant you stepped away from me, Jon walked back into the circle of students and we began.

Jon stared at me for a moment, and then turned his back. I waited a fraction of a second, then walked up to him, close, until there were just inches between his back and my face, then I moved a little closer, until the peaks of my breasts brushed against his T-shirt. He didn't move. I could smell him, he smelled like soap and laundry detergent. Clean, but with potential.

'Turn around.' I kept my voice low, controlled.

'No.'

Staying where I was, I ran my hand up his back, feeling his muscles tense as I found his shoulder blades and reached up over his shoulder, laying my palm flat at the top of his chest. He turned his head towards me, then away again. I could feel my breath begin to quicken as I remembered your instructions. Concentrate. Keeping my hand on his chest, I walked around to face Jon and, lowering my chin, I snapped my eyes up to meet his gaze.

'Listen to me. If you think hard, I know you can remember. Say it.'

'No.'

I could feel his chest rise and fall under my palm.

'Say it.'

He held my gaze and remained silent. Intense. His eyes were dark brown, flecked with amber and framed with long dark lashes. I faltered for a moment, and then spoke again.

'I know you remember, or you would have walked away by now. It's there, on your mind. You can still taste me on your tongue. I know you can. I haven't been able to forget that kiss. I can remember every second and when I play it through in my mind it's like running towards the edge of a cliff. I know you felt that. Say it.'

He opened his mouth a fraction and then hesitated, his gaze still locked with mine. It started to feel as though there was no one else in the room. Just him and me. And you. I slowly drew my eyelids down over my eyes and breathed in slowly, my body edging ever closer to his. I began again, a gravelly edge creeping into my voice.

'Your lips against mine, you couldn't help yourself, you pressed them to mine, you had no control, your tongue fleeting for a moment into my mouth, warm, you could hardly breathe, and I could feel you getting hard, I moved my hand down between us. Your breath caught for a moment. I know every fibre of your being wanted to fuck me then, like now. Your tongue probed my mouth like you wished your cock could my . . . mmmm . . . say it. Say it and it will happen. Say you want to fuck me.'

I don't know what came over me, but all of a sudden I leaped up and pressed my mouth to his, and we were kissing as though we were completely alone. His hands edged my shirt up and his fingers pressed against my naked back as I felt myself rise on to the tips of my toes in an effort to better force myself into the kiss. He stumbled backwards, both of us breathing hard, and all I could think of was how much I wanted to fuck him right then and there. I was so involved in it that I jumped when I heard you clap your hands together, and as we pulled away from one another

I looked around at the slightly stunned students and then my gaze met yours. You smiled at me for a moment, then nodded and moved into the circle to stand next to us. And just that one word.

'Yes.'

Jon and I dispersed back into the crowd of students, and the class continued. There was something so unexpected about the force with which I had played the improv, and what happened during the exercise lingered with me after the class finished. It was as though my attention had been focused entirely on it, directed, of course, by you. It must have lingered with Jon too, because as I was leaving the building and throwing up my umbrella against the half-hearted November drizzle, there he was, leaning against a wall near the exit. He called out to me and I walked over, already knowing exactly what the outcome of the evening would be. Did you know, too?

His hair was very short, but dark against his scalp with the rain, and his eyelashes seemed to frame his eyes even more emphatically as they clung together with water. His voice was deep; it seemed to rumble inside his chest before it escaped his lips. He asked me to go with him for a coffee at the Poets Café a short walk from college, and of course I agreed. We walked slowly, despite the weather, and didn't really say anything to one another, certainly not about the exercise in class. It felt good though, the sense of portent – the air between us was charged and even though we were virtual strangers, it felt right. There was a feeling of certainty in the unknown. It had been too long since I'd had that feeling.

We never made it to the café. Just as we were walking past a narrow alley near the high street, Jon edged me off the pavement towards it, wordlessly. It was barely wide enough for the two of us, just a space between two buildings really. Anyone wandering by, eyes cast down, eager to get out of the rain, would never have noticed us. But there we were . . . I'm only writing this here because something in me really does believe now that I should. That it's what you want from me . . .

Jon pushed me gently back against the wall, his eyes boring into mine. The half-light from the orange streetlight above us glinted off the amber in his gaze. The wall was damp, I could feel it cool against my back, even through my coat. But my skin was hot. His hands were against my hips, forcing them against the hard surface behind me with a subtle pressure, and he edged one leg, bent slightly, in between my legs. He leaned his forehead against mine, and then lowered his lips on to my mouth, pausing for just a second before dipping his tongue inside, fleetingly at first, then deeper. We both let out muffled moans to be connected that way again. I moved my hands up and slowly unzipped his jacket as we kissed, then broke away and began kissing his neck, hot and strong under my lips. I slipped my arms around his body underneath the shelter of his jacket, and I felt his hands move down my sides and slide my skirt up. I thanked heavens I had worn a skirt and no stockings. His hands were slightly cold, and this together with the sheer pleasure of his touch made me jump slightly as they edged up the outside, then slipped around to the inside of my thighs. They crept tortuously, following the dip in the muscles of my inner thighs, and he leaned his body forward against me to get a better angle. His chin rested against the crook of my neck, so I moved from his neck to take his earlobe into my mouth, sucking on it just as his fingertips met at the middle, between my legs . . .

His breathing quickened as he felt how wet I was, even through my panties. He moved against me, and I could feel him hard through his jeans. A loud gasp escaped my lips as he brushed ever so lightly against my clit with the tip of his index finger – even with the barrier of cotton it felt so intensely sweet to be touched there, in that way. He moved his fingers against me again, this time two fingers, lingering, finding the bump of my clit straining against the barrier of my pants and he began to rub slowly in circles against it. My mouth hung open in a silent groan, and he moved his face again in front of mine, his eyelids low, his eyes searching my face for flashes of increased pleasure, which they found as he rubbed harder, faster, over my panties, then I pushed my head back against the wall as his fingers drew the fabric aside and gently regained their position against my now naked pussy. I let out a long, strained mmmmmm and his fingers hesitated, teasing – he pulled them away, flickered back against my clit again for a moment, then pulled away again.

His fingers were beginning to get slippery, even before he took them away from my clit and pushed two fingers suddenly, deliciously deep inside me. His other hand supported his weight, his palm flat against the wall next to my head, his face right next to mine, but he wouldn't kiss me now, he just stared at my changing expressions, and my face contorted and I strangled another moan as he began to work his fingers inside me, sliding one against the other, slick with my excitement. He began to search around with his fingers and found what he was looking for with his fingertips, that perfect spot, ridged and raised, and his fingers began to rub vigorously against that sweet spot until I was breathing so fast I thought I was going to pass out, at which point, fingers still working inside me, he reached his thumb up to my clit and began to rub at that until my knees buckled and I came so hard I screamed, until his other hand rested softly against my mouth to stifle it.

As I began to recover I reached towards his belt buckle, eager to please him as he had me, but he held my hand and moved it away. Low, in my ear, his voice rumbled up even further inside his chest: 'I need to fuck you properly. How far is your place from here?'

I told him – ten minutes' walk. We got there in seven. As I fumbled at the door for my keys, he leaned against my back and kissed my neck, until I finally got the key into the door and could break away from him just in time before I gave up and fucked him right there on the steps. We practically ran up the flight of stairs to my flat, and as soon as we got inside the door I grabbed him and set to work taking off his jacket, his sweater and T-shirt, my fingers wrestling with his belt as he kicked off his trainers and stepped out of his socks. Finally I got his belt free and his jeans crumpled to the floor. I was still shrugging out of my coat as I led him down the hall to my bedroom, just barely registering that Vanessa didn't appear to be home before I pushed Jon on to the bed, his head and his cock both straining expectantly towards me. I paused, and slowly began to peel the rest of my clothes away from my body, still feeling the hum of the orgasm I'd had moments ago, my panties still damp. I left my bra until last, letting out a coquettish sigh as my breasts bounced free, before climbing on to the bed and straddling him, teasing for just a moment before giving in. We fucked for hours, and fell asleep in a naked, sweating, contented heap.

When I awoke this morning, we were still entwined, and I lay awake for a moment just enjoying the feeling of newness, of this strange man in my bed after so long. I had an odd feeling of ambiguity about the whole situation. It was abundantly clear that Jon and I were sexually very compatible, and we obviously had our acting interest in common, but I couldn't help thinking again that in some way the whole thing had been orchestrated – manipulated – by you. I did it, though, didn't I? I completed the class assignment. Top marks for concentration . . . And it's funny, because while it was happening, you didn't enter my mind once. But now, especially after getting this, the diary, back from you this morning . . . There you are again.

As we realized that the time was getting on for ten in the morning, Jon explained that he had to get home and get his kit for football, so I lay in bed and admired his form as he pottered about, picking up his discarded clothes from the floor. I noticed that Nessa's door was now closed and I could hear snoring even through that, so I guessed that Derek was back. It was nice to think that, for once, I'd had as much fun as she had last night . . .

When Jon had finished dressing, he came over to me and leaned over to kiss me goodbye, unexpectedly tenderly, on the forehead. He took my phone number and said he would see me in class if not before. I was relieved that it wasn't too awkward between us given the sudden nature of what had happened last night. I felt empowered and excited at the potential for something new. But still there was this niggling feeling of you over my shoulder, whispering in my ear. And then, suddenly – I heard your voice. You were at the door.

Jon was just leaving as you were putting my diary through the letterbox. Someone must have let you in as they were exiting the building. I was suddenly panicked, embarrassed – but also pleased. That you would know what had happened last night. I wondered if you might be jealous, or impressed that I had taken your task to its full conclusion, or surprised . . . I wasn't sure, but my entire body tingled at the knowledge that you were at my apartment, and there I was, naked in my bed. I heard you tell Jon that you were just dropping something off for me and then I heard him walk back in, obviously leaving my diary on the coffee table in the living room as you turned to leave. I couldn't decide whether to come out of my room and say something, but I felt paralysed. All I could do was listen and wait.

As you both left, I waited until I was certain I had heard the front door close and then pulled on a T-shirt and some underwear and wandered out into the hallway towards the living room. My diary was sitting on the table expectantly. I waited, my heart beating fast, and went into the kitchen to make myself a cup of tea. Then I went and sat on the sofa. I had seen it – the note – in a white envelope peeking out from between the pages. I pulled it out. On it was simply my name, written in bold capital letters in black ballpoint pen. 'TONI'.

The envelope wasn't sealed, it flapped open. I pulled out the note inside, handwritten again in small capital letters on a piece of lined paper, which I could see was torn out from the back of my diary. You had begun to write something and then scratched it out and started again:

~~I DON'T WANT YOU TO THINK THAT I~~
YOU ARE GOOD AT THIS. DOUBT IS ALL PART OF THE PROCESS. KEEPING IN TOUCH WITH EVERYTHING YOU ARE FEELING IS WHAT IT'S ALL ABOUT. YOU ARE RIGHT TO QUESTION THIS WHOLE EXPERIENCE. BUT IF YOU ARE WILLING TO STAY ON THIS JOURNEY THEN PERHAPS, IN THE END, YOU WILL UNDERSTAND THE REWARDS. OR YOU WILL HATE ME. I DON'T KNOW. IT IS UP TO YOU.

M

I read it, studied it, for what felt like an hour, going over it over and over again, the crossed-out part – why did you leave it? Why didn't you start a new page? The way you signed it – M – how should I perceive that? The way you wrote, what you wrote, I pored over it until I heard Nessa stir and begin to walk down the hall, at which point I stuffed it quickly back inside the diary and loudly proclaimed that I was going to have a shower. She eyed me with a look of curiosity mingled with the knowing twinkle of a woman who recognizes when a person has got laid.

But I was flushed not just from that, but from the whole experience of the past twenty-four hours. I felt as though something was growing inside me – like I was becoming more the person that I set out to be when I moved here. I'm taking risks, doing things I never would have expected I was capable of before. And then your note . . . I jumped in the shower, and felt awash with potential.

THURSDAY 30TH NOVEMBER
I haven't written anything else here all week. I feel like I've just needed to let everything sink in a bit. Jon and I went for some dinner the other day, and it was lovely. He was very sweet and walked me home, but wouldn't come in, saying he wanted it to be more like a proper first date. I have to say that I was secretly a little disappointed, but I know I will see him

tomorrow. And I will also see you. I am nervous and excited – the two things I am feeling with increasing regularity these days. I can't wait.

CHAPTER FOUR

THE MAGIC IF

It's a small word – if. But it has power. It is a key to a lock inside your head. It is a key that unlocks all that uptight bullshit that keeps the majority of the world enslaved to a pattern of so-called reality. Well, we deal in make-believe. I mean, you need to ask yourself: 'What would I do if I found myself in these circumstances?' You have to look at the parameters of the situation dictated in whatever you are playing, and then ask yourself that simple question. Doing so will unlock the door – it's permission to play adult 'let's pretend'. I mean, shit, let's face it – life is a series of choices, an endless series of decisions. Every single thing we do, everything we say, what we eat, how we get to work, who we fuck, fall in love with, whatever. It's all a choice. We balance on a knife-edge on a daily basis. And 'If' deals the cut. Do you understand what I'm saying? Now in our business, the writer has already laid out the environs, the scenarios, the words and the deeds. It is up to you to take that and ask yourself what would be necessary for you to carry out those actions, the actions of your character, in the circumstances dictated in the writing. It is important to be one hundred per cent honest with yourself in terms of your reactions, ask yourself the 'magic if' question, and then . . . act accordingly.

SATURDAY 2ND DECEMBER

I don't even know where to begin here . . . Just a few weeks ago, everything felt so routine, simple – I felt as though I knew what would happen on any given day. But now it seems that every moment is totally unpredictable. I just have to take each moment as it comes and feel my way through. It's kind of ironic that in last night's class we were talking about the Magic If – well, ironic under normal circumstances, perhaps. With you, I don't know what can be classed as irony, and what is manipulation. What is real and what is just a game?

Yesterday's class was the first one where I felt both completely out of my depth and at the same time felt like something was really happening in terms of my development as an actor. And, on reflection, as a woman too. For all the things that we had learned so far, really going up there in front of people and trying to use Goldberg's words was far more challenging than I had imagined it would be. I had thought that, particularly after what happened with the improvised seduction scene, and with Jon after that, I was ready to access the kind of sensuality necessary to play Angelique, but when it was time to read the words out loud, I froze. Somehow just reading her opening monologue, her detailing in such graphic language her exploits from the night before . . . Despite my desperation to sink my teeth into the part, I was shocked to find that something was holding me back. Which was odd considering how I'd spent my journey over to class last night.

I met Vanessa outside the tube and we made our way to class together. She had been working the late shift for most of the past week and so our paths hadn't crossed much at the flat – this was the first opportunity she'd had to interrogate me properly about what had happened with Jon. I felt a little bit irritated by the way she was bursting with pride at my having finally made some 'conquest'. After all, I wasn't a hermit, it was just that opportunity hadn't really knocked, not in any viable way, until he came along. But it was also quite sweet that she was so happy for me. I didn't want to tell her about how ambiguous I was feeling about the situation. But then again, talking about it again did heighten my desire to get Jon back into my bed. It was fun to relive it all, and describing it was like that sense memory exercise – it really did take me back to those feelings in a way that made me blush and lower my voice to a whisper as I described every lick and kiss and . . . Anyway, she of course made me tell her every detail of the night, and proclaimed loudly how jealous she was that I had managed to fuck the hottest guy in the class.

When we arrived, Nessa was still enraptured with my story and we carried on talking as we sat down. I was relieved to have an excuse to avoid making eye contact with you. Then Jon came over to say hello, and as he leaned over to kiss my cheek I saw Vanessa's eyebrows shoot up towards her hairline – I couldn't help but smile. But I also couldn't help searching the room to see if you had seen us. And there you were, you didn't even hide it – I looked up and you were staring at me with an unreadable expression. Then just as quickly, you turned back round and continued looking at some notes. Something about that moment made me not want to hand you the diary, not yet. It felt as though I was waiting for something to happen, I didn't know what, but something exciting. And it turns out I wasn't going to be disappointed…

As the class began, you told us about approaching the scenes, particularly in a challenging play like *Straight Through Sunday Blues,* with a view to examining how we would react if we were to find ourselves in the circumstances of these characters. When you told us that we could choose a portion of the play to work on, in my head I knew straight away that I would like to try the opening monologue. Of course, it crossed the minds of several of the other girls, but I was the first to volunteer to go up and do a reading. I knew the piece by heart, and as I walked up the steps at the side of the stage I was feeling ready to really show everyone, show you, what I could do, particularly after my display last week in class. But as people settled and I turned around, everything I had been working on went out of the window. I faced the front of the stage and started to speak, but it was as though my lips were frozen – my mind went blank and I could feel a searing heat creep up the back of my neck as embarrassment and frustration took hold. I could only bear the quizzical looks and mounting snickers for a few moments before I had to make a fumbled apology and leave the stage as quickly as possible. As I walked past you, your eyes followed me, and I heard you tell me it was OK, we all get blocked sometimes. But I was mortified and kept my gaze glued to the floor. I couldn't believe that for all the training we had done so far, and my bravado, that I had managed to mess up when it came time to prove myself. I knew I would have other opportunities, but never imagined they would end up presenting themselves quite so soon . . .

In any case, the minute I exited the stage, I heard Veronica Martin's voice volunteering to try it. My mortification increased tenfold. I knew she would make a meal of the speech – she was built for the part. I had thought that Nessa wore her sexuality on her sleeve, but Veronica almost put her to shame – she oozes confidence and her every movement drips with sensual portent. I sank into my chair as I watched her approach the stage, figure-hugging jeans clinging to what seemed like miles of lithe limbs, stripping off her cardigan as she reached it, so that by the time she mounted the steps she was dressed only in a cleavage-exposing black vest top. She ran one hand through her short blonde hair, pushing it back off her forehead as she turned to face us at the front of the stage, and set her lips in a knowing come-hither smile. She launched straight into the speech, and even though she had to glance down occasionally at her copy of the play, she was word perfect.

ACT I, SCENE I
New York City. Today. Night. Angelique Lakeman has just walked into her apartment. She leaves most of the lights off as she lives alone and prefers to feel her way around. There is an air about her that is almost feline, a feeling that all of her senses are heightened. She is overwhelming in her femininity and sexual presence. She walks into her kitchen and opens the fridge – her shapely frame is backlit by the light inside it. She pulls out a beer, pops it open, takes a long luxurious swig from the bottle, then turns around and begins to speak.

ANGELIQUE: That's better. Don't get me wrong, I love it at the time, but after a while you feel like you need something else in your mouth to take away the taste. But I always swallow, as a rule. It's better for them, and it's neater and more . . . complete for me in a way. I mean, if I was a guy and some girl spit out my cum I would be offended. And there's something of a metaphor in having a man's cock in your mouth – it's a perfect example of woman appearing submissive but really holding all the power. If you think I sound like I'm trying to justify something – I'm not. I don't do it for money or anything. But yes, here I am alone in my apartment. What are you thinking? I don't seem like I'm in love, do I? But I think I am. Now, that's new. The funny thing is, I prefer it this way. I'm glad that he's married to her and fucking me. Though he's probably fucking her too, I can live without the marriage part. And I'm not too proud to share. I don't know what her take on it is, but frankly I couldn't give a shit. All I know is that when I'm with him something inside me comes alive – and more often than not it's his dick.

[She chuckles.]

He loves doing it in their apartment. It's a little clichéd, but on the whole it works for me – hotels are bullshit, and I like to keep my own space my own. And in a way it feels special, him letting me into his home. Kind of like he's confirming my place in his life as a whole. I didn't believe him at first when he said that he loved me, but after a while I came to realize that it's more a case of feeling it than understanding it. I don't know if that makes sense to you or not. You know that phrase – making love. Having sex, making love. It's like we created it somehow between the two of us, we fucked so much we made a whole new feeling.

[She smiles a private smile.]

But here I am now, by myself. Which, like I said, is fine, but I do like to think about him, about what happened when we were together, live it all over again . . . Tonight, when I got there, it was really late – we only had twenty minutes before he had to go and pick the children up from their grandmother's. *She* is away visiting her sister. We're always careful not to make any grand displays of affection at the front door, but as soon as it closed behind us he swept me into his arms and we kissed hungrily. It was sweet that he tried to make it seem as though it was more than just grabbing a quickie where we could, asking me if I'd like a glass of wine. But I didn't answer. Instead, I backed him against the door, pulled up his T-shirt and began kissing his chest, biting it, licking it, and soon he reached up his hand and started playing with my breasts . . . I rarely wear a bra, especially when I'm going to see him, and so as he touched me my nipples stood to attention through the thin material of my top. He circled them slowly with his fingertips until I could barely concentrate. Then, using his other hand to raise my chin back up towards his face, he slipped his hand, warm and slightly rough, up over my stomach and on to my naked breasts, where he continued to play with my nipples as he kissed me deeply. We were both breathing heavily, and I broke away from his kiss and began to slip down his body until I was on my knees in front of him . . .

[She drifts off for a moment, and then walks over to a sofa and flops down on it. She closes her eyes, and begins to speak more as though she is talking to herself.]

I looked up at him and he put one hand on top of my head. I could feel the weight of it on there for a moment, the pressure on there, and that struggle of power, the struggle in his head between his basic desires and his wish to be a gentleman. We held each other's gaze for just a moment before he moved his hand down and smoothed my hair. I was almost disappointed that he wasn't more forceful. But I reached up and undid his jeans, and his cock popped out at me. I inched forward towards him, staring at his cock as I licked my bottom lip and glanced up at him again. I could see his chest rising and falling heavily. His hand was still on the back of my head, resting, and his cock strained towards me as he felt my breath against its tip. Then, ever so slowly, I edged my tongue towards it and began painting circles around the end. He tasted tangy and burning hot against my tongue. He let out a slow mmmmmm, which grew into a louder groan as all of a sudden I wrapped my lips around his cock and took it deep inside my mouth. I let my teeth scrape ever so slightly against the shaft as I sucked, starting to move rhythmically up and down, sliding my tongue around the length of him and tightening my mouth around him as I felt him grow inside it, felt the veins in his cock against the sides of my mouth. His hand gripped a bunch of my hair now, not too tight but tight enough that I could tell he was getting close, and he shifted his hips so that they moved towards me, and the tip of his cock was touching the back of my throat as I sucked harder and harder until he cried out and then panted hard and cried out again, and I felt a hot salty burst against the back of my throat as I sucked and then swallowed hard, swallowed all of him down.

[She pauses for a moment, exhales, then a broad smile spreads across her face. She opens her eyes again and speaks up, back out to the audience.]

And then I looked up at him with this grin on my face. And we started to laugh. God, I miss him already. But then, that's half the fun, right?

When she finished, she stood up and looked over to you for approval. You stood up and nodded your head wordlessly, a smile turning up one corner of your mouth. She seemed buoyed with pleasure and I could understand why. She was great. And I had failed miserably.

As class ended, Jon came over to ask if I would like to go for a drink, which I thought might break me out of my disappointment, but I knew I wouldn't be very good company and wanted to keep things good between us. I asked him to give me a call tomorrow instead. I obviously seemed miserable enough for Vanessa to offer to stay in tonight and have a girlie night in with some wine, ice cream and bad romantic comedies, but I sent her on her way. I knew she had more fun exploits to be getting up to. Instead, I lingered behind after class. I think I could almost sense that you were waiting for me too.

When the last person had left, I walked over to you. I needed some kind of feedback, some kind of reassurance about what had happened in class. I didn't quite know what I was going to say. But you spoke first.

'You look good enough to eat, Angelique. Let's get out of here.'

I thought I'd misheard, but you looked dead in my eyes and said again: 'What do you say, Angel?'

I was stunned for a moment, but the way you looked at me filled me with confidence in a way I have never experienced before. I understood what you were doing, and I surprised myself by slipping into the role. Her voice just escaped from my lips.

'I'm ready when you are, sweetheart.'

You paused for a split second, your eyes searching mine. Then you grabbed my hand and we strode side by side out of the building. As we walked through the door, you let me walk out slightly ahead of you and, edging your body close behind me, you slid your hand around my hips and tapped my bottom gently. I somehow managed to maintain my composure, remembering I was Angelique now.

I turned to you with a sly smile and breathed, 'Hands to yourself there, sugar.'

You grinned a mischievous grin and took my hand again as we walked out on to the street. I wasn't quite sure where we were heading, but all I really cared about at that point was my hand in yours and that feeling I had when you looked at me. Angelique or Toni. I couldn't tell if you were in character too, which of us it was that was causing that gleam in your eye that seemed like it was reflecting a heated glare of sex. I felt powerful and gorgeous. Before I knew it, we had reached a cluster of bars, and you were opening the door to a dark establishment I had never been in before, although I remembered walking past and thinking it looked expensive.

The interior was all red and black, and there was subtle, bass-heavy music playing in the background. We walked in and went over to the bar. I leaned forward against it coquettishly, undoing my jacket so that my shirt, unbuttoned generously low, was exposed – and so too was my cleavage. You slipped a hand around my waist and rubbed my lower back in small circles beneath my jacket as I winked at the barman to get his attention.

'Hey, doll – could I get a beer, and whatever he's having.'

You ordered a bourbon, gulping half of it down before the glass had barely touched the bar. The smell of the alcohol mingled with your warm scent. You smelled just like I imagined you would, clean and musky all at once. I breathed you in as you leaned over to me, electricity sparking down my spine. You nonchalantly brushed the hair back off my neck and kissed me right at that soft spot below my ear, next to my jaw. I held my breath as you pulled away, lingering close to me until I finally turned away towards the barman, who had coughed politely and told me the total. I cocked a thumb towards you.

'He's the money, sugar.'

Then I turned and pulled out my compact, reapplying my lipstick in the mirror as you paid and picked up our drinks. But as we walked away from the bar, instead of heading towards an empty table you walked over to a beautiful red-haired woman who was sitting by herself near the window. I had noticed her when we walked in, felt her eyes on us, but I hadn't given it a second thought until . . .

'Marguerite.'

There was something about your tone of voice, a note of affection, of anger, of something I couldn't quite place. There was so much history just in the way you said her name. She looked up at you without smiling. She had huge, stunning violet eyes, and although she looked older than me, possibly nearing forty, she had an air of sophistication that would be immediately attractive to anyone with eyes and class. You stared at one another for what felt like an eternity. Then her eyes darted over to me. She looked me over slowly, and I felt at once defensive and somehow ashamed. At last she spoke. Her voice was smoky, deep.

'Hello, Marcus. Thank you for coming. Who is this?'

She kept her tone even, but I could tell that it was a struggle. I felt used and ridiculous, and the minute the two of you had locked eyes I began to think of some kind of excuse so I could get out of there. But before I had a chance to speak, you spoke.

'This is Angelique. Angel – this is Marguerite. My wife.' You seemed to say that deliberately, then hesitated for a moment. 'My ex-wife.'

I had no idea what to do. And then you looked over at me, and there was a sense of pleading in your eyes that I couldn't escape. You needed me to be that girl, and I couldn't understand why, but something in me just couldn't walk away from you. You needed me.

'Marguerite. It's a pleasure to meet you. Hope we didn't keep you waiting too long.'

I gave you my best desirous look and shimmied in front of you to squeeze past and around the table, brushing my arse exaggeratedly against your crotch. Marguerite stared at me with barely hidden displeasure. I shrugged off my coat and sat down opposite her, flicking back my hair. You took the seat between us and rested your hand on my knee, which was bare as I hadn't worn tights again, despite the cold. A tiny, appreciative smile played at the corner of your lips. Then you turned back to Marguerite and said, 'What was it you needed to see me about?'

There was something so pained in your voice, and you were looking so directly into her eyes every time you spoke, and she into yours, that it took all my power to remain 'in character' and not jump up and leave. There was something so intimate between the two of you that made me well up with jealousy, despite the obvious acrimony. But you had brought me there. Why? I didn't have time to think about it then. I just had to look at it as another assignment. Stay in the moment and do my best not to freeze again like I had earlier.

Marguerite looked genuinely hurt by the way you were behaving, and after a while it seemed she couldn't stand to hold your gaze any longer. Looking down at the table and fumbling to pick up her handbag, she said that it didn't matter any more, she would just go. But you wouldn't let it drop.

'No, I'm here now. I'm all ears, Marguerite. What is it you wanted to say?'

She stood up, shaking her head and smoothing down her dress. She had an incredible body, like a 1940s movie star. I could see you were affected by her, by the way she looked. Your eyes travelled all around her, scanning her. Then back up to her eyes. She looked as though she was searching for something, like she didn't know quite what words to use. I felt sorry for her, but at the same time jealous, and as Angelique I couldn't help myself.

'Look honey, you can say whatever you want, it's OK. I'm not selfish, we can share.' And I curled my lips and raised one eyebrow up at her as I reached over to fondle the hair at the back of your neck. Both of our eyes were trained on her. She sighed and shook her head again. Your hand tightened against my knee, as though you were trying to support yourself as finally she spoke again.

'Marcus . . .' she began, and then trailed off, as though she had changed her mind about what she was going to say. 'Marcus. I just wanted to say . . . I do love you. And I'm sorry.' Then she turned, picked up her coat and walked out.

My hand slipped away from the back of your neck as you sat wordlessly, gazing out of the window. I didn't know what to say. You had a small frown on your face. Your jaw was clenching and you were breathing heavily. I wanted to take your hand, still resting on my knee as though you'd forgotten it belonged to you, squeeze it, and ask you if you were all right. But just as I was trying to formulate a sentence, you turned and looked at me. The frown was still knitting your brow, as though you were trying to figure me out, as though you were surprised all of a sudden that I was still there at all. Then, using the hand still on my naked knee, you uncrossed my legs. You leaned towards me almost imperceptibly, and your eyes locked into mine. Your hand moved a little further up the top of my thigh, until the very tips of your fingers just barely slipped under the material of my skirt. I couldn't speak, couldn't look away. My lips parted slightly, involuntarily, and I felt my chest rise and fall at an increasing pace. And . . . you were just touching my thigh, but my pussy swelled with every passing second you stared into my eyes, your fingers tickling the skin just under the edge of my skirt.

And then, as though in slow motion and fast forward at the same time, you reached towards me with your other hand, skimming my jaw line and knitting your hands into my hair, you pulled me towards you and your lips enveloped my mouth in the most beautiful kiss I have ever experienced. As our mouths met, you breathed in hard through your nose, and there was an urgency in you, your entire body tensed and relaxed, tensed and relaxed as our tongues mingled and our eyes squeezed hard shut. I could taste bourbon and you and it was the most delicious taste, your hand roamed in my hair and I slipped my arms right around your neck, pulling you as close to me as I could with us both sitting on black leather chairs. I slid towards you and your hand moved further and further up my skirt, your fingers slipped around my hips and under the elastic of my panties. We kissed for what felt like a lifetime, we didn't care who was watching or what it meant or . . . we just kissed and kissed . . .

Until, all at once, I had to stop. I couldn't breathe. And all I wanted was you inside me. I broke away, panting, and started to stand, I wanted to leave and go somewhere, anywhere, with you. But you slipped your hand out from under my skirt and smoothed it down, resting your hand on my leg for a moment. I hesitated, and then sat down again. Your eyes wouldn't meet mine. You turned away from me and downed the last of your drink.

'Toni, I'm . . . I'm sorry. Look, let me . . . let's get you a cab.'

You stood up, but I felt frozen out once again. I wasn't Angel. Toni had to go home. I wasn't moving, so you said again, 'I'm sorry . . . come on –'

But I cut you off.

'No. Don't worry.'

I pulled on my coat and strode out with as much pride as I could muster. I wanted to crumple to the floor. But I left you standing there, and as I passed the window I could see you watching me, your mouth slightly open as though there was something you were about to say but couldn't. I got to the bus stop and wanted to cry but something wouldn't let me. Because what had happened felt incredible.

SUNDAY 3RD DECEMBER

I can't stop thinking about you. And I can't even begin to understand what happened on Friday night. I just keep playing it out in my mind, and I know you were there but can you understand . . . I mean, I don't know why but here I am writing in this fucking diary, I've written everything down here and yet I am absolutely nowhere in terms of knowing what you are thinking, what it is that you want from me. Why did you kiss me like that? And why did you make me pretend to be her? Did you think it would be easier for me, easier to make me . . .

Why is it that I can't just stop doing this? I feel like I don't have a choice. If I'm honest. I can't help myself. And you are obviously stronger than me but . . . I miss you. Friday evening is my favourite time of the week. You're making me . . . grow and do things that I never expected and I'm . . . grateful, and angry, and confused.

CHAPTER FIVE

OBJECTS

Where was your focus though? That's what I mean, you lose concentration and then it all goes to shit. I know it's late now, but you need to stay focused here, otherwise it's a waste of all our time, and mine especially. I'm sure as hell not up here for my health. You need to choose an object, something to focus on that will help you stay in the scene. It doesn't matter what it is, it could be your character's embarrassment, or the gun he's holding, or Ms Martin's décolletage – Lord knows, it's vying for your attention. Anything – imaginary or real, tangible or intangible. Grab hold of it with your mind and don't let go. And then you will be unshakable, and entirely real. OK – Jon, Veronica. From the top.

THURSDAY 14TH DECEMBER

It's been a while since I've written in here, I know. Even after class on Friday, I just couldn't bring myself to pick up a pen and write down what I'm feeling. Maybe I don't really know yet. And it's been a long time since you've read what I've written here. It just hasn't felt right to hand it over, and yet I keep writing. I can't really explain why . . .

But I've had a good week, I've had a lot going on to keep my mind off things . . . off you. Although, truth be told, this whole situation is never very far from my thoughts. Actually, it's kind of funny that we were working on 'objects' in class on Friday. Vanessa and I went for a girlie shopping trip over the weekend and it really did help. She was looking for some sexy lingerie to celebrate her and Derek's one-month anniversary. It seemed a little premature to celebrate the relationship to me, but for Nessa one month was quite an achievement! As we trawled around the shops, I watched her try on umpteen bras, panties, teddies, suspender sets and even a nurse's uniform. It felt very odd to help another woman pick the outfit that she would use to seduce her man, but it was a welcome distraction. Nessa knew something was up with me, and as we hung out in the changing rooms, the whole story of what happened between you and I last week came tumbling out. I stopped short of telling her about this, the diary, though. Somehow it felt too private to talk about. What I write on these pages is for you, and it's for me too. But no one else.

She was flabbergasted, and quickly voiced both her jealousy and anger. She was, however, impressed that I had been able to keep in character – at least until the kiss. I feel an odd sense of competition with Vanessa, especially when it comes to playing Angelique, as she is perhaps a more obvious choice. And it also bothers me still that she thinks of me as someone who is not quite in touch with her sexuality.

I do think that there is mounting evidence to the contrary, and with some of what has happened lately, I have to admit that I have surprised even myself at some points. For example, as we wandered around one lingerie shop, I grabbed Nessa's hand and led her downstairs. We were both giggling and teasing one another, but as we approached the bottom of the stairs and saw the displays, we fell silent.

All around us were row upon row, shelf upon shelf, of sex toys. There were handcuffs and cock-rings, love eggs and dildos galore. We looked at one another and smiled, then laughed, and Nessa exclaimed, 'Excellent!' I knew she already owned at least one vibrator, but I had never had one – it was something I had always wanted to try but never had the guts to go into a shop and buy one. We walked over to a display of them, and I was amazed by the assortment. A shop assistant wandered over to us; he was quite handsome but very disarming and surprisingly helpful. He told us to hold the testers up to our noses to feel the varying speeds of vibration. I soon found one that I liked – it was electric pink, not too fussy but I knew it would do the trick. Nessa picked up some kind of remote-control vibrating bead, the control for which she planned to present to Derek as part of their celebrations. We paid for our new toys, and I just couldn't wait to get home and have a play.

Vanessa was working the night shift on Saturday night, so as she scurried out of the door, late as ever, she gave me an exaggerated wink and told me to have a nice time. It was funny, the anticipation of using it was already turning me on, and without ever having you cross my mind. Instead, I put on some music and ran a bath. I added some lavender oil and settled in for a long, luxurious soak with some candles and a glass of wine. It felt great to have some 'me time', and just relax.

After my bath, I dried off and slathered my body with lotion so my skin was soft and silky smooth. I slipped on my satin robe, the one I usually only wear if I have company. Tim had bought it for me as part of a birthday present once. It felt comforting to wear it, and reminded me of the feelings I'd had at the time. It was all so much less complicated then! I settled on to my bed and pulled the vibrator out of the drawer in my bedside cabinet. My body felt primed with anticipation.

I slipped some batteries into it, and felt it come alive in my hands. I switched it off for a moment, and lay back on my bed on top of the covers. I turned off my bedroom light so that only my dim bedside lamp remained. I could see myself reflected in my dressing table mirror, and it took me back to Friday's class, to the object I picked to focus on in the scene. Angelique's compact mirror. We were playing the flashback scene when she first meets David and they are in the bar, like we were last week. I decided to use her mirror as my 'object' upon which to focus because it somehow felt appropriate. Staring at myself in its reflection, pretending to be her, helped to force me into being another person, watch myself change before my own eyes. Which is, in a way, how it feels writing in here. Reliving everything that is happening to me, putting it down on paper, is starting to feel like a learning process. I do feel angry, manipulated in a way, but I also appreciate what it is that you are trying to do – or at least what I think you are doing. I don't know.

Watching myself as Angelique also awakened something in me, the same thing I felt lying on my bed and watching myself that evening – a realization of my potential as a woman, as a sexual being. I've felt sexy in my life, of course, and I know I'm attractive, but really watching myself, I really did feel beautiful, desirable. Is that how you see me? I think – I'm beginning to think – it might be.

But for that night, lying on my bed, I didn't have to think about you to climax – I didn't have to think about anything. I nestled my head on the pillow and bent my knees so that my feet were flat against the mattress. I gripped the warm rubber vibrator in my hand and turned it on. I loosened my dressing gown, the satin cool against my skin. I put it on 'gentle' at first, and edged it gradually up my thigh, and then used the tip to tickle my bottom where it touched the mattress. Then I angled the shaft and went for the plunge – I inched it inside me, deeper and deeper, until only the controls remained outside of me. It felt incredible. I moved it in and out of me a few times, then pulled the length of it out of my pussy and rolled it around the lips, up and down. My hips writhed against the mattress, and I moved the vibrator up until the tip touched ever so slightly against my clit, which stood to attention. I gasped at quite how powerful it felt – the feeling was like nothing any man had ever provided, no matter how skilled a lover. I pressed it against my clit again, switching the vibration speed to high, and could barely catch a breath before an enormous, shivering great orgasm shattered my entire body. I cried out and touched the vibrator against my clit, and came again. I don't think I've ever come so hard in my life. It was fantastic.

But, even though I didn't have to fantasize or think about anything sexy at all to reach such a strong climax, I did feel something missing. That warmth of another person. Still, it was exactly what I'd needed at that point, and I fell asleep feeling satisfied and refreshed. Like you said in class – focusing on that one object really did help me keep my concentration and accomplish what I had set out to, and it felt really good.

FRIDAY 15TH DECEMBER

I woke up early this morning, like I do every Friday – I know class isn't until the evening, but somehow my mind needs a lot of preparation time before Friday night comes around. I know it's been a while since I last gave the diary to you. I wasn't really ready for you to read it, especially after last week. And looking back over it – so much has happened since the last time you read it – everything with Jon, and what happened last week . . . But I plan to hand it over today and you can take a look. Maybe you could drop it by tomorrow? I would really like it if we could talk . . . about this, about class – about everything. Anyway, I'm late for work, so I'll stop now.

CHAPTER SIX

SUBSTITUTION

That was fine, Toni. Look, we all get stuck sometimes, you're almost there. It's just a question of using the tools we have available to us to help overcome those problems. Remember the sense memory exercise, using those feelings to access something real in a scene. You need to take those principles and apply them to your scene partner sometimes, but instead of your senses you can substitute whoever is in front of you for somebody else, someone who you can picture in your head who will inspire the feelings appropriate for your character in the scene.

You know, if I need to create a fireball of hatred towards someone then I know exactly who I would substitute in my mind and it will come across . . . And if I needed to create a feeling of desire, or I needed to think of someone who would. . . you know, make me feel . . . give me a little confidence if I felt I was lacking it. I know . . . I know who I would choose to think about. So, yes. Substitution. Try it. I think it might help. OK? Now do it again and make me feel it.

SATURDAY 16TH DECEMBER

I know things in my life have taken a strange turn ever since I moved here, but yesterday's class really did surpass anything so far in the craziness stakes. I mean, first of all there was your little pep talk. In class, I've been so used to you berating us, that for you to actually try and make me feel better about how badly I was doing in the scene was odd. And the things you were saying – something about it felt personal, or at least more personal than the pointers you were giving the others. I don't know though, maybe I'm just reading more into things. But the way you looked at me when you were describing the people you would conjure up in your head in order to access certain feelings in a scene with a partner – I could tell you were talking about Marguerite. And I think you were also suggesting that, maybe, you might think about me . . . ?

You said there was a particular person you would substitute in your mind if you needed to feel a boost of confidence. Someone who would create a sense of desire in your mind . . . The confidence part I guess I can understand, particularly after yesterday. It's embarrassing if you think . . . well, I've already told you that your opinion matters to me, and I guess it's no secret that I find you attractive. In any case, ever since we went to that bar . . . I thought things between us were ambiguous before, but now I'm more confused than ever. And then there was what happened in class, and then this morning . . .

Even though I have (obviously) still been writing in here, it had been a long time since I'd had the courage to give you the diary. And you hadn't asked for it, either. I was beginning to wonder – well, more like worry – that you didn't want to carry on with this exercise, or whatever it is, any more. I hadn't had a chance to give it to you on that Friday before we went to the bar . . . and then after that I had been avoiding you so it was only yesterday that it seemed right to hand it over again. I was worried about you reading all the things I've put down in here since you last read it, but at the same time there was that eagerness again – I needed you to know everything that I've been feeling over the past few weeks.

I got to class a little early and when I walked in you were the only person there. You were sitting on the floor leaning against the stage with your legs stretched out in front of you, making some notes. I stood by the door for a moment watching you, and every so often you would lean your head back against the edge of the stage, thinking about something, before scribbling more notes. Then you noticed me standing there, and we just looked at each other for a while, before a smile spread across your face. I couldn't help but return it. I started towards you, but then two more students brushed past me and went and sat down. They were chatting amongst themselves and not paying us much attention, so you got up and I walked over and held the diary out towards you without saying anything. Without looking down at it, you took hold of the book and for some reason I didn't let go, we just stared at each other. Then you said hi and, kind of hesitantly, asked me how I was, at which point I broke away from your gaze and looked down, letting go of the diary.

'Oh. I'm fine . . . you know.' I was tongue-tied. Luckily Nessa walked in at that moment and waved me over. I was relieved but my heart was beating so fast just at that tiny exchange between us. I hoped you couldn't tell. Well, at the time I did. But here I am again, telling you. I don't know what it is that you do to me but somehow I end up telling you everything through these pages!

Anyway, we settled into class, and you told us that you were going to divide us off into pairs again to run various scenes from the Goldberg play. I was half-hoping I would be paired off with Jon again – if nothing else, I knew we had chemistry and I really wanted to prove myself this week after having choked up last time I tried something from the play. But, much to my confusion, you paired me with Vanessa. And the very part of the play I was least prepared to perform was, of course, the one that you picked for us to tackle. You obviously hadn't given up on testing me. I wasn't sure, as ever, what your intentions were, but I was determined, despite my anxieties, to give this the best possible shot that I could. I wasn't going to let you faze me.

Yet, even with my strong desire to prove myself, the first time we ran the scenes was a disaster. And yet you were kinder on me – on us – than you were on some of the other pairs as we moved off into separate areas to rehearse. I could hear you stopping people halfway through, with your trademark 'What was that?' I half-smiled, but I panicked because I knew that any moment you would come round to Nessa and me and we would have to run through what we had been working on. I was very flattered, however, that you had told me to read Angelique and Vanessa to read Lydia's part. It seemed like an odd choice, especially given that Nessa hadn't really had a chance to shine in class as yet, and she certainly seemed like an obvious contender for the Angelique role. I could tell she was pissed off too, but both of us were eager to please, and doubly as eager to prove ourselves.

Nevertheless, it was a struggle for both of us, not least because of the requirements of the scene. It was tough enough with it being the part of the play where Angelique breaks it off with her married lover and, in a bid to take her mind off things, ends up staying late after work at the bar and going home with a woman that she has been serving drinks to all night. But being told to play the scenes with Vanessa felt even stranger – I didn't realize then quite how strange it would get, but in hindsight, perhaps I shouldn't have been surprised . . .

ACT II, SCENE III

Mitchell's. It's late. The bar is almost empty. Angelique is coming to the end of her shift. A woman who has become something of a regular – Lydia – has been sitting at the bar all evening, alone. She has offered to buy Angelique a drink. Although she is tired and looking forward to her bed, something about Lydia draws Angelique in. Lydia is beautiful, voluptuous and has a voice like honey. So, despite herself, Angelique agrees to pour them both one for the road.

LYDIA: What's your poison, darlin'?
ANGELIQUE: Whisky. Straight up. What can I get you?
LYDIA: Well, a woman after my own heart. I'll have the same.
[Angelique pours two generous glasses of whisky and hands one to Lydia. She leans over the bar towards her.]
ANGELIQUE: You're always here alone. I think that has to be a choice on your part.
LYDIA: What makes you say that?
[Lydia smiles, runs her tongue along the edge of the glass to stop her lipstick smudging, and takes a sip of her drink.]
ANGELIQUE: Am I wrong?
[Lydia shakes her head and smiles, her eyes locked into Angelique's.]

ANGELIQUE: Like you said – a woman after my own heart.

LYDIA: Absolutely.

[Lydia raises one eyebrow suggestively.]

ANGELIQUE: So, do you often ply women with drink and try to get them to play?

LYDIA: Only when I can't help myself.

ANGELIQUE: I should be flattered then.

LYDIA: Flattered, maybe. Or you could just enjoy making a fool of me.

ANGELIQUE: No, I wouldn't enjoy that, sugar. Not one bit.

LYDIA: But I'm not your type.

ANGELIQUE: Well, I'm not a stickler for tradition.

LYDIA: Then let's get out of here.

[They hold one another's gaze for a moment. Then Lydia downs the rest of her drink, and looks up at Angelique with a glint in her eye. After a moment's consideration, Angelique does the same. Lydia slips suggestively off the barstool and Angelique follows behind her. The lights dim.]

It was awkward at first running through the bar scene with Nessa, and we hadn't even got to the scene in Lydia's apartment yet. We couldn't stop giggling and had to start again. It only got worse when you came over to watch us, and I was embarrassed that you had singled me out for the 'substitution' tool, but after you spoke to us, when we ran it again I could definitely sense an improvement. Substituting . . . making Lydia's character into someone else, somebody I could relate to being attracted to, really did help. When we finished, there was a strange, palpable sense of attraction between us – it was more intense than I expected. I had always thought of Vanessa as sexy, but in my head as we ran the scene, the boundaries were starting to blur, between her, in front of me, and . . . you, in my mind.

You looked from me to Vanessa and back, nodding almost imperceptibly. It was then that you told us to go up on the stage. Both of us hesitated – it had felt good, but we didn't think we were ready to play it in front of everyone and be critiqued yet. But then you walked over and pulled the curtains across the front of the stage. You walked back over to us and in a low voice said . . .

'Stay focused.'

People looked a little curious, but you just went back to mingling amongst the students working on various scenes, giving them pointers about the script or blocking or how to approach the writing, for what felt like an age. Nessa and I walked up the steps, parted the curtain aside and stood behind it. With the heavy velvet material separating us from the rest of the class, it felt very different. Intimate. The sound was dulled, and it was dark back there – the only light came from the gaps at the top of the curtain and the tiny space where the curtains met. We didn't say anything to one another. An odd tension still remained between us. Then, after what seemed like an eternity, you suddenly appeared from behind the curtain. You walked past us into the shadows and returned dragging an old sofa that had been left backstage from some play or other. You pulled it in between us, then stepped back into the darkness. Then, just your voice.

'OK. Begin.'

Vanessa and I looked at one another, and I could tell immediately that she had slipped into the character of Lydia. Her eyelids drooped low, her gaze sensual; she ran her tongue subtly across her bottom lip and rested one hand on her hip. Just as quickly, I felt Angelique take over. There aren't many lines in the scene – which is part of why it is so challenging to play – but I could remember the ones that there were with ease, and so could Vanessa. It was as though we were channelling these characters, and you were there in the dark, watching it all take place. She began:

'Well, this is it . . .' She undid her jumper and let it slide down her shoulders and arms and on to the floor. I eyed her steadily. Then, wordlessly, we walked towards each other and stood in front of the sofa but, before we sat down, I reached up and cupped Nessa's chin with one hand. I stepped closer to her, so that there were barely inches between us, and before

I could even think about what I was doing, I pressed my lips to hers. I felt her lips, slick with red lipstick, slide against mine. After tensing for a moment, she put both of her hands on my waist and slipped one leg around the side of me and one in between my legs, so she could press her body against mine. Although I knew it was Vanessa, something about that moment, with you watching in the shadows, made it feel as though somehow it wasn't just her, but also you that I was kissing – it was incredibly erotic, and before I knew it, Vanessa and I had fallen back on to the sofa.

Her hands slipped under my T-shirt and over the sheer, silky material of my bra. I pulled away for a moment, suddenly remembering my line, as though it was a thought from my own head.

'Well, you have a beautiful home.'

She grinned, and wrapped one leg around my waist. I slipped my arms around her, her hands still under my T-shirt, and, in spite of myself, I felt my nipples harden as she eased the material down and freed my breasts without undoing my bra. I looked into her eyes but they weren't Vanessa's, they were Lydia's . . . they were yours . . . I felt dizzy. I kissed her again and ran my hand along the thigh that she had pressed against my side, and around on to her bottom, moving away from her mouth to kiss her neck. I knew we were going much further than even the script dictated, but I felt as though I couldn't stop. My fingertips dug into the flesh of Vanessa's arse, and I could hear her breathing hard, her breath coming in warm bursts against my ear. She was wearing tights and a jersey dress that was basically a large T-shirt. She had cupped her whole hand over my breasts, her hands were burning hot, and I reached down between her legs – she was damp even through her tights. I knew I was too. It was impossibly sexy and I didn't have time to think about what we were doing because as my hand reached down to her pussy, she inched forward and began to grind against my fingers, her lips parted in a silent moan. I pressed them against her and she sighed quietly, obviously aware somewhere in the back of her mind that there was a class of students on the other side of the curtain. I began to move my fingers faster and faster, her hips moving quicker and quicker back and forth until she froze and I felt her entire body shudder.

She collapsed against me for a moment, both of us breathing hard. Then, her voice muffled against my shoulder . . .

'Fuckin' hell!'

She pulled back and looked at me, then burst out laughing. I smiled. I had never experienced anything like that, and never thought it would happen under those circumstances, that's for sure. Still, if it was with anyone, it had to be Nessa. We clambered up off the sofa and straightened ourselves out. She still had a wicked grin on her face as she picked up her jumper, made her way over to the steps and parted the curtain. Perhaps she had forgotten you were still there – but probably not. She bent forward, tousled her hair exaggeratedly, then whipped her head back and winked at me before walking back down.

You emerged from the shadows and walked over to me, so close that my heart started to beat even faster than it already was from what had just happened. You stood in front of me, and looked as though you wanted to say something but couldn't. You just leaned over and tucked a stray hair behind my ear, then let your hand rest against my cheek just for a fraction of a second. Then you left.

I had almost forgotten that I had given you the diary, so it was a bit of a shock when, lying in bed this morning at eight o'clock, unable to sleep despite having a Saturday off for once, I heard a knock at the door. It was quiet at first, and I didn't want to get up because I presumed that, at that time of the morning, it was probably one of Vanessa's gentleman callers, sneaking back for more or to pick up something he had forgotten. Things had gone straight back to normal, and there was no awkwardness between the two of us, which was good. But then I remembered she had planned to go over to Derek's after her late shift at the restaurant so, grudgingly, I rolled out of my nice warm bed. It was only when I got to the peephole and peered through that I remembered you were going to drop the diary off today. I panicked, because I saw you begin to reach down for the letterbox to drop it in and turn away. I made a frantic effort to wrestle my curls into a bun and pulled open the door. You looked up and smiled. The cool air against my legs reminded me I had slept only in a particularly short T-shirt.

'Hi . . . thanks. Thanks for, um, bringing this by.' I took the diary from your hand and stood staring at you. You looked as though you had just got up yourself – you were unshaven and, despite it being winter, you wore only a thin jumper against the cold. It looked soft though – I wanted to reach out and feel it. Thinking that made me smile, and you smiled back again.

'No problem – I was off to get the paper anyway. Sorry it's so early.'

I told you it was fine, I wasn't asleep. You seemed to be peering past me, probably checking to see if you could detect Jon's presence in the background. I didn't want you to think he was here, so although I panicked the minute the words escaped my lips, I asked you if you wanted to come in for a cup of coffee. You paused, and I could tell, well, I think you were tempted to say yes, but after a moment you made your excuses and turned to leave. But I lingered for a moment at the door and you turned around again and walked back towards me.

'Toni . . .'

I felt all the blood rush to my head. I didn't know what you were going to say or do. I braced myself. I can still remember every word.

'I'm sorry about the other week. It wasn't my intention to upset you. I was being selfish. I just . . . it meant a lot to me that you stayed. I didn't really expect you to. And I know you think that I'm unpredictable but . . . well, you have not failed to surprise me yet. I wanted . . . well, I wanted to say thanks and –' then you stopped short. My breath caught in my throat. Then you began again, in a low, intense voice.

'And I just wanted to say, before I go, that . . . that you look stunning. I thought it was bad in class, but it is taking every ounce of strength I have to not take you into that apartment and fuck you right now.'

I stood there, taken aback. Your eyes bored into mine, and I almost dropped the diary, which I was still clutching. Before I could say anything, you turned around and walked away down the hall.

I thought I might still be dreaming. I made a strong pot of coffee, sat down and started writing in here again . . .

CHAPTER SEVEN

PRIVATE MOMENT

OK, this is important . . . Because sometimes it's easy to forget that what is happening on the stage should be completely and entirely separate from what is really going on in the theatre. The audience doesn't want to be reminded that you are just some bloke on a stage trying to pretend you're somebody else. Every moment you spend on the stage should appear to be private to the audience. We've already worked on how you can get yourself into the moment as an actor, but to those people watching, you have to draw them in – you don't go to them. They have to come to you. What you're doing on stage has to be so intimate, seem so personal, and yet they are captivated – they can't look away.

And that's something that I want you all to work on today. I need you to think of something that you would only ever do if nobody were around, something totally private that you couldn't imagine doing in front of anyone else. Use what we've been working on, create a private space in your mind and then go for it. And then you're going to do it in front of all of these good people . . .

FRIDAY 22ND DECEMBER
The minute I started I knew you wouldn't let me get away with it. Something in your eyes when I got up

on stage . . . I mean, nobody was really doing anything ground-breaking. A couple of people picked their nose and ate it, which was already more than I really wanted to see! One girl talked to herself, as though she was having a real conversation with what turned out to be her dead aunt. Nessa struggled with the task, as there was genuinely very little she could think of that she would do in private that she wouldn't do in front of others. But she settled on plucking her bikini line with a pair of tweezers. I couldn't help but laugh.

But it was strange, sitting there in class, just another of your students, after what had happened last week. I've been finding it hard to fall asleep without thinking about it, replaying everything you said in my mind. On the one hand I've been counting the seconds until I could see you again, but on the other, and especially once the time came and I was sitting in front of you, I was panicked, wondering what might happen. My worst fear was that you would ignore me, and act as if you had never said those things to me. Unfortunately, at first anyway, I was right. When I walked into class, my eyes shot straight over to you, and I sat down right in your eye line, but you carried on chatting to one of the other students. Just before class started, you did look up at me and make eye contact, but there was not so much as a smile or a nod of acknowledgement. I was devastated.

When it came time for me to do my 'private moment', I decided to do something that I genuinely had never done, in my adult life at least, in front of another living soul. I sang. And not just a quiet little tune to myself – I performed a full-on show-tune, as loudly as I possibly could, my voice cracking terribly on every high note. I felt a mixture of embarrassment, hysterics and pride that I had even managed to go through with it. I finished with an exaggerated flourish, and began to giggle as soon as I reached my conclusion. Everybody clapped, but you just stood, wordless and with a small frown knitting your brow. But even though I knew that what I had done was a bit of a cop-out, I still felt a pang of frustration at your lack of encouragement.

It felt like an eternity until class ended, and I was really desperate to get out of there as soon as I could. I asked Jon if he would like to go and have a drink after class, but he had to work the late show at the cinema that night, and get up early in the morning to go to his other job at the hospital labs. We hadn't seen nearly as much of one another as I had hoped we would – we were both busy and I guess my mind had been on . . . other things. But I was disappointed not to have something I could escape off to – Nessa was on the evening shift too. I suddenly felt very lonely, and as I gathered up my things, I was beginning to feel very sorry for myself at the prospect of another

Friday night on my own, in front of the TV, eating ice cream . . . But then I looked up and you were standing over me.

I looked around and pretty much everybody had left. A couple of the girls were chatting by the door, but after a moment they continued on outside. And it was just you and me. I felt defensive after what had happened in class today, but you looked down at me, and there was something hesitant, almost vulnerable, in your voice as you said 'hi'. Part of me wanted to just get up and walk out, steer clear of any further trouble. But there was a much bigger part of me that wanted to leap up and stick my tongue down your throat. Neither of those won though. Instead, I mustered a solemn 'Hello', and stayed sitting, clutching my bag and coat. You didn't seem to know quite what to say next, and so you just stood there for a while, with your hands in your pockets and your head hung down, looking at me with those big blue eyes. Finally, I broke the silence.

'I know that wasn't really my best work, I just –'

You interrupted.

'No. No, it was fine. It was just that . . . well . . . It didn't really feel honest, that's all.'

'Honest?' I was on my guard again. I was tired of hearing you talk about honesty when you couldn't seem to be totally honest with me about what it is you are doing with this whole 'exercise'. A silence hung between us again for a moment. But then you said my name. Toni. There was something in your tone that reminded me of the way you said Marguerite's name at the bar. I melted. It felt wonderful to hear you say my name like that, pleading, affectionate, frustrated. And that edge of desire to your voice too. I conceded.

'I know. I know what you mean. It's just hard to really . . . I don't know, I couldn't think of how to really put across that idea of privacy in the context of the class, I just –'

'Show me now.'

I looked up at you, and there was something in your eyes that told me exactly what you meant. I sucked in a deep breath. I didn't want to ruin the moment, to spoil the chance for something truly intimate – private – between us. And I knew I was powerless to resist that look, the look you give me sometimes, it does something inexplicable to my insides, they leap and swirl and something shoots straight through me, from the top of my head down through the centre of me, down into my . . . it turns me on in a way that I had never experienced until I met you. I didn't know quite what to say. But I gathered my composure. I put down my coat and my bag, and then stood up, my body only inches away from yours.

'OK.'

I lingered there in front of you, and tilted my head up towards your face. Our lips were almost touching;

I could feel the air stirring between us as our breathing quickened. I looked all around your face, studied every eyelash, watched you pull your bottom lip in between your teeth, and close your eyes, watched your nostrils move as you breathed me in. I suddenly felt powerful. I leaned ever so slightly closer to you and whispered in your ear.

'I'll show you now.'

I walked over to the stage and pulled a stray chair to face it. Then I walked over to the door, pushed it shut and locked it. I flicked the light switch next to the door-frame and the room fell abruptly into darkness. The only light was coming from a couple of stage lights that dropped pools of amber on to the wooden platform; the rest of the stage was cloaked in black. I cocked a finger towards you and then pointed at the chair in front of the stage. You paused for a moment, then walked towards me and sat down, stared at the stage, and then back up at me. I was wearing my black leather boots, which had quite a generous heel – I had had to convince myself to buy them at the time, they felt a bit too outrageous, but at that moment, they were perfect. One hand had somehow found its way on to my hip, and I stood off to the side of you, hip pushed out to one side, and a smile curling one side of my mouth. You shifted slightly on the plastic chair and folded your hands conspicuously in your lap. But the devilish smile on your face was more than enough to spur me on.

I walked past you, slowly, and swung my hips exaggeratedly as I mounted the steps to the stage. It felt like the dark denim of my jeans was clinging to every curve. As I moved towards the centre of the stage, all I could hear was the clop-clop of my heels against the wood, and our breathing. All else was completely silent, and there was an almost cavernous echo to the space. I stood directly in front of you on the stage and held your gaze for a moment, then walked off into the darkness, returning with another chair, which I placed exactly where I had been standing, only a foot or so from the edge of the stage.

I sat down on the chair and crossed my legs. Then slowly, deliberately, I unzipped the boot on the leg resting on top. I slipped off the boot and my stocking underneath it. Then I crossed my legs the other way and did the same with the other boot. I placed them neatly next to my chair. The stage was cold against the soles of my feet. I stood up and turned around to face the chair so that my back was to you. Then, again slowly and deliberately, I unbuttoned my jeans and slid the zip down. I turned and looked over my shoulder at you. Your eyes were locked on to me. I turned back round and eased my jeans down over my hips and down my legs, bending over to slip them off each foot. I straightened back up and folded them over the chair. Then I sat back down, made sure you were watching me, and then began to unbutton my blouse, one button at a time, as slowly as I could. I slipped out one arm, then the other and, again, hung it on the back of my chair.

I was naked, save for a sheer bra and panties. The cheap plastic chair was as cool as the stage floor against my skin, but I didn't feel the cold. On the contrary, the look in your eyes was making my pulse quicken with every passing minute. I sat still for a while, just soaking in that feeling between us. And as we sat there, looking at one another, something began to take over me – my hands became your hands. We were several feet apart, but with you looking at me the way you were, it was like you were willing me to do the things that I began to do.

Without looking down, I raised my hand – your hand – towards my face, and ran a finger across my lips. Then it slipped inside for a fraction of a second, and tickled the tip of my tongue, then back out and across my lips again, moistening them ever so slightly. And then that hand continued downward, fingertips skittering down my throat, until it rested flat against my chest, warm, my heart pounding underneath. It rested there, and the other hand ran along my thigh, along from my knee, skin smooth under its touch, slowly feeling its way along until it rested at the top of my leg, then snuck down in between. I pulled my knees together and squeezed that hand in between my legs, trapping it for a second, with the other hand rising and falling under the weight of my breath.

I held that hand between my legs, motionless, for as long as I could, until it struggled to be free – your eyes prised my legs apart again, though I resisted, they slowly, ever so slowly, moved apart. The hand cupped my pussy greedily, fingers wriggling, feeling for something. My – our – other hand slipped down my chest and on to one of my breasts, and they both seemed to swell at the touch. Fingers wriggled under the material of my bra and took one dark, yearning nipple between thumb and forefinger, causing a small sigh to escape from my lips. The hand between my legs grew more fervent, and my legs began to move further apart, giving it more room, then our fingers pulled aside the material of my panties and, starting at the back, two fingers slid up and down just inside my pussy, back and forth, back and forth, slower at first but gathering pace. My legs were as far apart as they could go, the fingers of the other hand still playing with my breasts. My hips began, involuntarily, to grind back and forth on the chair in rhythm with the fingers in my pussy. It was only then I realized my eyes were closed – I had felt so enveloped in your gaze that I hadn't noticed. I opened them and looked down at you.

Your eyelids were low, and you began to shift in your seat, almost in tandem with me. I began to groan, and the sound echoed all around. Without warning, the fingers inside my pussy slipped up and over my clit, slick with my excitement, and then back down inside, along and back up over my clit, and again, again, again, then they stopped moving back and forth, they just stayed around my clit, slipping and sliding around and around it, up over it, rubbing it harder and harder and harder, the other hand grabbing and kneading at my breasts, and I threw back my head and cried out hoarsely as I came, feet scrunched up on to the tips of my toes, my hips thrust backward, and as I brought my head back down to look at you I noticed a damp pool on the chair and on the floor in front of me. Still cupping my pussy in one hand, my body continued to spasm and, as you gazed up at me, I could see that your cock was straining up at me under your trousers. You were panting hard, but not moving, your forehead creased with a furrowed brow. Your hands were gripping the sides of your chair. But you wouldn't move.

I began to recover, pulling my legs back together and readjusting my underwear. After what felt like an eternity, I could see the muscles in your body begin to relax, along with the front of your trousers. Your brow remained furrowed, and I could see your jaw clench and unclench. It was as though you wanted to say or do something but were forcing yourself not to. I had seen the look before. Despite the intensity of what had just happened, I suddenly felt utterly deflated once more. I turned around and pulled my blouse off the back of the chair, doing it up as fast as I could, then I stood up and put my jeans on, avoiding eye contact. I picked up my boots and dragged the chair back off into the darkness. I sat back down on it under the cover of the shadows and pulled on my stockings and boots. Once again, I felt entirely powerless. I didn't know what to do. I could see you, still seated in front of the stage, your shoulders hunched and one hand on each of your knees. You looked angry – I wasn't sure at what. Maybe at yourself.

Then that echoing clop-clop again as I walked off the stage and down the steps.

'How was that?'

You didn't answer, and the sarcastic tone in my voice felt ugly. Something in your demeanour made me feel sympathetic towards you, rather than the anger or violation that it seemed I should be feeling. During the whole . . . performance . . . you just sat there. You didn't do anything, you didn't move towards me, you didn't try to . . . But, in that moment at least, I didn't feel angry. Instead, I touched your arm. Then I gathered my things, unlocked the door, and walked out.

SUNDAY 24TH DECEMBER
Christmas Eve. I'm heading home this afternoon. I've

needed a couple of days to really digest what happened on Friday night. It almost feels like my weeks are just a bland blur of days, and then every Friday something happens that turns my world topsy-turvy again. But in any case, I feel like I'm ready to move on. I need to get past this and just work on me. I don't know how much longer I can keep doing this. But I am anxious at the same time to know how you are, and to let you know that I'm . . . OK.

I am kind of dreading going home, though. I feel so much a part of this city now; my life is here, my work, Ness and our flat. You're here. It will be strange, seeing Mum and Dad, and thinking about you and what I've been up to since I moved out. And seeing Tim too. That will perhaps be strangest of all. Despite – or perhaps because of – all the mind games and the trials and tribulations that I've gone through in your class, I do feel that I am an entirely different person to the one that was in love with him. I don't know what we have, but it's so far removed from anything I have experienced before that the girl from those times is like an alien to me now. I know I'm growing, slowly but surely.

That doesn't mean that I'm not frustrated, at your inaction, at your game playing. I'm angry at the fact that I pour out my feelings to you in this fucking thing, and yet you remain unattainable. I almost feel like your resistance to me is punishment for being so direct in here. But then again – just like I can't stop writing, you can't seem to stop spurring me on, as much as you want to keep a distance from me, you can't seem to help but invade my space. I don't know what will happen in the New Year . . . But, in spite of myself, I'm looking forward to finding out.

CHAPTER EIGHT

MOMENT TO MOMENT

Are you OK? Yeah? OK. Then why the hell did you stop? So you fell over the chair, so what? Just because something unexpected happens doesn't mean that everything has to grind to a halt. Do you think you could get away with that in front of an audience? Of course not. You would have to keep going. And don't just pretend that nothing happened, as though they wouldn't notice the fact that you've just tumbled to the ground if you jump up fast enough . . . Use it. Use that new opportunity that has been presented to you in the scene. Nothing is set in concrete. You're trying to conjure up something real and tangible, and life is full of obstacles and surprises, at the risk of sounding trite.

I mean, the whole point of this scene is that the two of you are having an argument, which you are losing. So you fall down. Stay down, you're defeated. Deliver the rest of your lines from the ground. That would have been perfect. You should be praying for accidents like these to happen, you know? I mean, if you're on that stage night after night doing the same fucking thing over and over again, you're going to go out of your tiny little minds. Have some bloody balls in this game. OK?

SUNDAY 7TH JANUARY

New year. Everything feels new. This has to be the most surreal . . . I don't really know what I'm going to write. You've just left. And immediately this is what I think of to do. I'm beyond questioning it now though. Just let it happen, and go with the flow. That's basically what you were saying in class on Friday, right? It's kind of ironic now, looking back. Anyway . . .

I dropped the diary through your letterbox on the Sunday before I travelled back down to my parents' house for Christmas. Nessa had seen you going in to your place a few days before that, and came home all excited, telling me she knew exactly which house you lived in now. I tried to stay calm but I was also very glad that she had found out – it had been quite awkward you knowing where I lived, but me not really knowing where you might pop out from unexpectedly as I ambled home! When I went to drop off the diary, I could see a light on but I scurried away as soon as I had pushed the notebook through the door – I didn't want to risk having to talk to you after what had happened after class that Friday.

And when I got back to London on Wednesday, you had returned it. The diary was lying on the mat by the door. I had no way of telling when you had dropped it back, as Vanessa was still away. There was no note, nothing. And more importantly, I had no way of telling if you had even read it. I was confused, and a little upset. I flicked through the pages in case I had missed something, in case you might have written something at the end after my last entry. But there was nothing. My brain was telling me that I should just take it as a sign that this whole thing was over, that I should stop writing in here and move on, finish off the last few classes left in the course, and then focus on becoming the best actor that I could be. That is why I had left the safety of my home, and taken all these risks. To pursue my dream. My dream wasn't to be manipulated by some inscrutable man who couldn't face up to the fact that he was all mind games and no real action. But something else – not quite my heart, not entirely just my sexual desire for you – still wouldn't allow me to let it go. And so, in spite of myself, I was anxious to see you again in class on Friday.

I had arranged to meet Vanessa outside the tube station after work and head to class together, but she was late, so by the time we arrived you had already begun. We walked in sheepishly, and you looked up with an irritated frown on your face – hardly the impression I had been hoping to make. I was angry with Vanessa for being late – I had hoped to be able to have a chance to speak to you before class began, ask if you had read the diary . . . ask what you thought . . . I just wanted to have contact with you again, find out whether I should just give up. But in class, once more, you seemed to studiously ignore me. You did seem angry though, as if something was playing on your mind and your patience was thin.

I was hoping to catch you for a moment after we finished that evening, but Jon intercepted me before I could get over to you. He was looking even better than I remembered, it has to be said. He told me he had been to South Africa with his mother over the holidays, to help her get over her recent second divorce. He looked tanned, healthy and extremely sexy. He said he would like to make it a New Year's resolution to take me out again, and perhaps see if we could make a go of things. As he spoke, I felt rude as I kept looking over his shoulder to see what you were doing, and just as he asked me if I would like to go to dinner on Saturday night, I saw you look over at us, then pick up your case and walk out of the door. I sighed audibly in frustration. But Jon didn't seem to notice. I looked back at him and he was watching me expectantly, waiting for my reply. I smiled, and said of course. He seemed like a far better, more realistic opportunity for some companionship on these lonely London nights, waiting for the summer to come.

On Saturday afternoon, I went out and braved the sales to buy something to wear on my date with Jon that evening. I chose a black wrap-around dress that accentuated my curves and provided a generous glimpse of my cleavage, which was especially prominent due to some new underwear that I had also treated myself to. I wanted to look as sexy as possible, and really make an effort to get things off the ground with him – for my own sake as much as anything. The way you were acting in class made me certain that in the long run it would be better for me to draw a line under what had happened with you, and move on. I vowed not to continue writing in here as well. But that was before what happened that evening . . .

Jon was a few minutes early. I was still getting ready, so I yelled out to Nessa to open the door to him. She scurried in to my room having let him in, shaking her head. I asked her what was wrong, and she told me I was 'luckier than any fucking girl deserved to be'. After emphasizing her point by letting me know that, were it her, she wouldn't bother with the date part and would instead just bring him straight to bed, she bustled back out of the room and let me put the finishing touches to my outfit. I stood in front of the mirror and slipped on the most vertiginous heels I owned. I knew I looked good. And when I walked out and saw Jon, I felt immediately that I had made the right decision. He had on what must have been his best suit, dark grey, with a crisp white shirt open at the collar, which offset his newly acquired tan. He was carrying a single red rose. Vanessa was right – it was almost too much to take. I smiled, popped into the kitchen to put the rose in some water, and then we were on our way.

The restaurant was in an area of West London that I could barely afford to breath air in. Jon was really pulling out all the stops, and I was very flattered at his efforts. He pulled out my chair for me, and asked if it was OK for him to choose a wine. He was scoring points at every turn! The décor was beautiful, intimate candle-lit tables and couples huddled together, talking intensely. I was starting to berate myself for focusing so much on you to the detriment of my possible relationship with Jon when almost on cue . . . you walked into the restaurant. My heart almost stopped. The waiter had just come back to the table to take our order, and I could barely concentrate on the menu as I watched you out of the corner of my eye. You hadn't seen us, and I was straining to see who it was that you had walked in with. And then I saw her. I was absolutely mortified. You had brought Veronica. From class. It took me completely and utterly by surprise. But there she was, looking totally stunning while you took her coat. Jon turned around to see what I was staring at and, just at that moment, Veronica looked up and saw us. She leaned over and said something to you, and you turned around to look.

I didn't know what else to do, so I made a half-hearted wave. You both smiled weakly. Jon turned back around to me and asked if I wanted to go over and say hello, but I shook my head. You had gone back to chatting with Veronica, almost as though you had barely noticed us sitting there. My heart was pounding, but I genuinely didn't want to ruin my evening with Jon, so I did my best to concentrate as he asked me about how I thought the class was going, what my plans were for when the course finished in a couple of weeks, about my work at the bookshop and so forth. It took a lot of effort to keep chatting with him, all the while feeling your presence like a heat in the corner of the room. I kept looking past Jon's shoulder, checking if perhaps you were looking over at us, trying to decide whether it looked as though you and Veronica had been out before or if this was your first date. I couldn't tell, but your body language suggested that you were both very much at ease with one another. I was a ball of envy.

Eventually, our meal came and it was delicious enough to keep me focused for a while on the date I was on – that is until Jon began to ask what the situation was between you and me. He asked me if I felt uncomfortable with you there, and whether anything had happened that he should know about. I didn't know how to answer him. I was becoming less and less certain myself. I couldn't bear the curious look on his face though, so I excused myself to go to the ladies. I honestly didn't realize, however, that in order to get there I would have to walk straight past your table. I steeled myself to say hello but, just before I got to the table, you also got up and walked towards the cloakrooms. I hesitated, but I couldn't turn back and sit down, so I said hello to Veronica as I walked past. She looked me up and down and half-heartedly returned my greeting. She had the hint of a satisfied smirk on her face. I headed quickly into the ladies.

When I came out, it seemed almost inevitable that I would walk straight into you. Literally, smack-bang into you. I stepped back and apologized before I realized who it was I had collided with. My face began to get hot, and I smiled at you with as much dignity as I could muster. It felt odd, being closer to your shoulder height, with my heels on. You smiled back and said, in that deep, searching voice – 'Hi'. We stood facing one another for a moment, then you stepped aside to let me past. I did my best sultry walk as I made my way back to Jon at the table; just before I sat down, I shot a glance over to see if you were watching me walk away. You were . . .

By the time we were ready to leave, Jon and I had relaxed into the date a little more – we had polished off the better part of two bottles of wine, as well as cocktails after dinner, which had helped greatly in allowing me to get over the fact that you were there in the restaurant, on a date with some other girl. We had lingered over dinner long enough, but now I was ready to have him take me home and stop talking, to start doing. In fact, it was only as we got up to leave that I noticed your table was empty, the waiters clearing it away ready for the late rush. I looked around, in some ways relieved, then I saw you standing outside the restaurant window with Veronica, waiting to hail a cab. Just at that moment, Jon arrived back from asking the hostess for our coats. And once again, I felt distracted as he helped me put my coat on and held the door open for me as we left.

I don't know why it would surprise me that you were hailing a cab together, despite the fact that Veronica once told me she lived in Clapham – not on the way to our neck of the woods by any stretch of the imagination. I wished I could stop feeling jealous and enjoy my time with Jon. But the more I thought about him, the more I kept comparing him in my mind to you. And although Jon had proved to be a great lover, and I really didn't know . . . then . . . what it would be like with you, there was some power you held over me that drew me to you in spite of myself. An air of mystery, a mean streak, but coupled with a strange vulnerability. I couldn't resist it.

We walked outside and there you both still were. It was heading towards midnight, and competition for cabs at that hour was beginning to get fierce. I tried to start walking a little distance up the street from you in order to avoid contact, but Jon had already begun walking towards you with a little wave, to say hello.

I followed reluctantly behind. The minute we stood next to you, Veronica looped one hand into the crook of your arm, with that same self-satisfied look on her face. I kept my hands studiously in my coat pockets, protected against the cold night air. My cheeks still felt hot, from a mixture of alcohol and embarrassment. Jon began to make small talk, while both you and I looked around anxiously for a cab. One approached, and we both stepped instinctively towards the kerb to hail it – it stopped before it got to us though. Suddenly we were slightly separate from Jon and Veronica, who were chatting away amiably.

I kept my eye on the oncoming traffic for the possible rescue of an empty cab as you began to chat to me like a stranger. It's a great restaurant, isn't it? Did you have the medallion of pork? It was fantastic, melted in the mouth. I nodded and smiled and responded monosyllabically, but then I felt words begin to bubble up inside me that I couldn't keep down. Suddenly, but in as low a voice as I could muster, I heard myself ask you what you thought you were doing. You looked at me with genuine surprise at the almost vicious tone to my whisper. You said nothing. I revised my questioning, in the same hushed tone, the alcohol giving me bravado I wouldn't have otherwise had –

'What do you think you're playing at? You continually make me look like a fool, then bring that slapper to some la-di-da restaurant when you actually want to get laid, right? I'm just for playing games with, right?'

I surprised myself at the forcefulness with which it came spilling out of my mouth. You looked at me with a frown, squaring your shoulders as if ready for a fight. 'Look', you said, then halted suddenly, adjusting your tone to match my own. Neither of us wanted to draw the attention of the other two. You started to speak again, but I cut you off.

'Did you even read it? The diary, did you even read it?'

Your eyes drilled into me, and you glanced up towards Jon and Veronica to make sure they weren't listening in, before moving a step closer to me. I could see the breath tumble from our mouths in clouds of cold smoke that dissipated into the air between us. Your collar was turned up against the wind and it played with your hair as you moved to stand in front of me. My hand, which I had left in the air awaiting the opportunity to attract the attention of a taxi, slowly wilted by my side as I looked at you. You had never looked sexier. You began again in that low voice.

'Toni, my week is not complete until I read what you have written. Of course I read it. Did I want something simple tonight? Yes. I wanted to move on, start again. Is that what you're doing with rent-a-hunk over there?'

Your eyes were searching mine, eyebrows still knitted together in a frown. We stared at one another until Jon's voice broke me out of my reverie – 'Quick, there's two coming!' He rushed towards us, flagging in a rather comical manner and ruining the suave impression he had been building over the course of the evening. I couldn't blame him – the wine and cocktails were swimming around in my head too, and making it hard for me to focus. Before I really knew what was happening, and with not another word between us, Jon whisked me into the front cab, and I saw you and Veronica bundle into the one behind it.

As soon as we got into the cab, Jon began to kiss me, but despite being up for it earlier, I just couldn't get in the mood. I kept thinking about what had just happened between you and me, and try as I might to enjoy what was happening, it was hopeless. Jon sensed my lack of enthusiasm, and collapsed back against the seat of the cab. He agreed that maybe neither of us were in the right frame of mind that evening, and asked if I would like to have the cab drop me at my place. It was very sweet of him to resign himself to my change of mood, and I thanked him profusely for the wonderful dinner. I felt awful for letting him – and myself – down.

The apartment was still and quiet when I came in. Nessa had left a note saying she was going out clubbing and not to expect her home. I was almost tempted to try her mobile and see where she was – the prospect of retiring to bed to sober up alone was frankly more depressing than I was ready to deal with. I wandered into my room and kicked off my heels, slid my feet into my slippers and, still clothed in the black wraparound dress, made a coffee and plonked myself down in front of the delights of late-night television. I must have almost dozed off, because the sudden tap on the front door made me jump. After regaining my composure, I tiptoed rather anxiously up to the peephole, half-expecting to see that Nessa had forgotten her keys, or perhaps it was Jon come to check if I was OK. The last person I expected it to be was you. I pulled back from the hole with a start, smoothed down my hair and straightened my dress, then looked again. It wasn't a figment of my imagination. It really was you.

Panic set in as you tapped at the door once more. I hesitated, and then moved away slightly and shouted, 'Coming'. I could feel the blood pumping in my temples. A thousand different questions seemed to whirl around my head as I tried to think of what it was you might want – whether you were angry, whether I should open the door at all. I waited as long as I possibly could before finally opening the door, just barely remembering to kick off my ridiculous fluffy slippers as I did so. You looked almost surprised that I had actually answered the door. But you can't have expected Jon to be here, otherwise what hopes could you have had . . .?

In any case, after an awkward, shuffling silence, you said hello. I said it back, and then, in my best effort to convince you I was still angry at our tête-à-tête on the street, I asked what you were doing here.

'I don't know.'

The tired, irritated, almost sad tone to your voice really got to me, but I tried to keep up a façade of anger.

'Barbie's gone home then, has she?'

'And what about yours, then? Look . . . Toni. I didn't come here to . . . do this. I just wanted to . . . I don't really know. I shouldn't . . .' You stopped. You had been avoiding my eyes while you were speaking, but now you looked directly at me.

'Do you want me to go?'

Those last words hung in the air like dark ripe grapes on a vine, ready to be plucked. You were looking into my eyes. So you knew what my answer would be. I stepped aside and you walked in. I closed the door behind you and turned around to face you again but you had wandered away, roaming around the living room but not settling. You still had your dark coat and suit on, and I could see your irises glinting blue off the low light of the table lamp. You continued moving around, slipping into the darkened kitchen. I followed you and stood in the doorway.

'Can I get . . . Would you like something to –' but your lips on mine cut me off before I could finish the sentence. Your beard was beginning to come through again – it was nearly 4 a.m. after all. Delicious prickles pressed against my cheeks as your mouth enveloped mine. Your hands slipped around my waist and I stumbled backward against the doorframe. Every muscle in my body felt like it was melting, my legs turned to jelly. You moved your hands up my body until they rested just below my breasts. My hands were in your hair, then down your neck, then pulling at your coat, your jacket, prising them down and off your shoulder and arms to the floor, then pulling at your shirt, reaching my hands down the waistband of your trousers to untuck it. You pulled back from the kiss and took a deep breath as you felt my hand brush against your cock. You were already hard. You reached up towards my face and cupped it in both your hands, then, when your face was inches from mine, with a look of supreme concentration, you licked your lips and placed them gently on mine again. I could barely breathe. Your tongue began to slip in and out of my mouth, with painstaking deliberation, fleetingly at first, but as you began to lose a little control, you kissed me deeper and deeper, and my breath began to catch. You stopped again.

I leaned against the doorframe again – the force of the kiss had drawn me away from it towards you.

The wooden frame nestled in between my shoulder blades as you pulled just my hips towards you. Your jaw clenched and unclenched. You wound the end of the tie that held my dress together around one index finger, grinning. Then, with one sudden motion, you pulled it and my dress fell open, exposing my intricately laced bra and panties. You made a strange, guttural noise at the back of your throat, and the grin still spread across your face as you began drinking in my semi-naked form. I shifted my weight from side to side, rocking my hips back and forth. I picked up the loose end of the tie and began to swing it gently between us. You caught the end and I pulled you towards me again. As we kissed once more, your hands slipped up and brushed the dress off my shoulders. The cool wood kneaded my now-naked back as you pressed your body against me. The feel of your cock against my pubic bone made me moan through the kiss, and you pulled away again. I could feel my entire body quivering with anticipation, before you put your hands on my waist and silently turned me around.

Again, you pressed your body against mine, the hard flesh of your cock straining against the expensive fabric of your suit trousers and into the soft pillow of my bottom. My lips parted in a noiseless moan. I felt your hands at my bra and then it suddenly popped free, and the lace material was replaced with your hands, hot, not quite soft, rubbing slowly and deliberately against my nipples, then down over my stomach and slipping roughly and suddenly down inside my knickers. I groaned, and writhed my arse against you. You made a muffled sound, then quickly spun me back around to face you. I couldn't keep still, I could feel my wetness slick the inside of my thighs as I rubbed my legs together, squirming under your grip as you took my hands and, with one of your own, held them together at the wrist. Your other hand travelled down my arms, my neck, my chest, over my breasts and down my stomach, then pulled my panties, already only half-clinging on over my bottom, down until they skittered to the floor around my ankles.

You let go of my wrists, but I left my arms stretched above my head, fingernails digging into the wooden doorframe. My breasts stood to attention, and my nipples strained towards you. Then you slowly, very slowly, began to slide your body down mine, your tongue moving first to my earlobe, then down my neck and chest. It caught and encircled the peak of one breast, and then followed a path down towards my navel. You were kneeling in front of me, your shoulders rising and falling with each deep, steady breath. And then, almost nonchalantly, you picked up one of my legs and rested it over your shoulder, bent slightly at the knee. You pulled my hips towards you and then . . . and then there it was again. Just the very tip of your tongue. You let it linger, the very tip of your tongue against the very tip of my clit. I stopped breathing. You pulled your tongue away for a moment, and then it was back, licking in long, luxurious strokes along the lips of my pussy, dipping inside and then slipping up over my clit, circling it with short, hard bursts, then slower gentle flicks, and then back along the length of my pussy lips again. You began to lick harder and harder as I got wetter and wetter and your whole mouth slipped all around my pussy which felt so swollen and hot but you wouldn't stop, you sucked my clit gently in between your lips, then pulled away just a fraction, blowing against it, I had never felt anything like it, then back between your lips, your tongue playing against it gently, and my legs began to shake, I could barely balance on the one foot still flat on the floor. I began to gasp short sharp bursts of air into my lungs, my hips thrusting backward and forward uncontrollably, your tongue pressing in tighter and tighter circles against my clit inside your mouth until I came with such a force that I collapsed on to the floor next to you, but you moved away so that you were still eating my pussy as my body was racked with pleasure again and again until finally you stopped and we both lay panting on the cold tiles of the kitchen floor.

But we weren't finished yet. After waiting a while to regain my composure, I stood up and looked down at you. I was entirely naked and you were not. I needed to rectify that. I reached one hand down towards you and whispered, my voice still raw from the orgasm – 'Come here'. You stood up and wrapped your arms around me. Your cock was still impossibly hard. I reached in between us and unbuttoned your shirt. You were slender but there was far more in the way of toned muscle under there than I was expecting. My pussy began to swell again as I ran my hands across your chest. You shrugged out of the shirt. My hands were already at your belt, and in a moment your zip was undone and your cock sprang out at me. I was surprised – you had no underwear on. I smiled from ear to ear. Your cock was absolutely perfect. Just as I had expected. You stepped out of your trousers and I backed you against the sofa until you sat down with a soft thud.

You stood straight up to attention as I straddled you as slowly and seductively as I could, arching my back, one leg on either side, my knees sliding into the meeting point between the seat of the overstuffed sofa and its back. Rivulets of sweat were dripping from both of us already, and as I edged my hips closer to your cock, we both began to breathe faster, not wanting to rush but not being able to help it. You grabbed my bottom with both hands and squeezed it hard. I raised up slightly and hovered for as long as I could stand it, poised to take your cock inside me. I lowered myself ever so slightly, until the opening of my pussy, still slick, just touched the tip of your cock. Although you were looking into my eyes, the second you felt the moisture against your cock, your eyes squeezed shut, and your lips parted slightly.

I tried to hold off, but I could hardly wait any longer – I let my weight press down and envelop your cock in me, warm and moist. You let out a load moan that just turned me on even more; I began to grind vigorously against you, one hand gripping the back of the sofa for leverage. The sound of you inside me was incredible; I had never heard anything so dirty. You squeezed my arse with one hand, and a breast in the other, a series of strangled gasps emanating from you as you leaned forward towards me, your body beginning to tense, and I tightened my grip around your cock with all my might. The sensation of using the muscles in my pussy like that brought on a succession of orgasmic waves that coursed through my entire body, and seemed to explode at the very moment that you shot your warm cum into me. I felt completely and utterly spent.

We collapsed into an embrace, you still inside me, and held one another for a while before we finally let go. We must have fallen asleep for a while, but when we awoke, the sun was coming up. Instead of making excuses to leave, you gathered up our clothes, and I smiled sleepily as I watched your bottom wend its way towards my bedroom. We slept all morning, and then had some toast and coffee for breakfast. We didn't talk much, about the class or what was happening between us. At that moment, we were just content. And then you left. I know you were there, but it just feels so right to relive it all again in here . . . it always has. Writing it down and letting you read it makes it all the more real, makes it something more . . .

I know we don't have a plan. You seemed anxious to avoid making any grand statements about the future. I don't think I'll even see you again before next Friday. I simply don't know. But what I do know, Marcus, is that I have never been fucked, or fucked with, so well.

CHAPTER NINE

JUSTIFICATION

You have to get more into it, really commit to it. Yes, you will look like a fucking idiot but that shouldn't be too much of an issue for you lot. You really need to throw yourselves around completely randomly, really go for it. And when I say freeze, I will point to one of you and you will have to justify why you are in that position. As in . . . 'Well, Marcus, my hand is there because I'm a vet and I'm castrating my husband's cat, wishing it was his balls that I had at the end of this scalpel.' Or you're . . . I don't know, you're seeing if it's really possible for you to get your own cock in your mouth. Whatever, you get the idea. You have to justify the reason you are in that position when I tell you to stop. OK? Go.

SATURDAY 14TH JANUARY

I can't believe it's been a week since I last wrote in here! It has been very hectic this week – especially with taking a couple of Vanessa's shifts at the restaurant as she has gone on a short break with Derek – they seem to have lasted! Well, at least as far as her relationships go, they have. And I really needed the money after Christmas. But coupled with work at the bookshop, I've been literally gagging for my bed by the time I get home at night. And yet here I am, first thing on Saturday morning, when I could be sleeping in, I feel the compulsion to write in here!

It was nice to see you on Wednesday, though. I'm only sorry it was so brief – I would have liked to see more of your house . . . your bedroom, perhaps? But still, we made a pretty good go of things against the wall in your living room. There was something great about that, it felt naughty and illicit, but so comfortable – well, as comfortable as it could be, fucking against a wall. I keep remembering getting the giggles when you nearly dropped me and I had to grip on to the edge of the sofa with my toes! It makes me laugh and turns me on at the same time. People keep looking at me like I'm some kind of weirdo on the bus! But I can't help thinking about it. About you.

I wish I hadn't had to run off to the restaurant that evening. I just needed to drop off the diary, and that was the first time in the week I had walked by and your light was on. I couldn't bear to just drop it through your letterbox without the chance of seeing you again. And it felt more important than ever, you reading that last entry about us . . . It doubles the pleasure, writing it and knowing you are reading it. It's a huge turn-on that I've never wanted to admit fully, but once again, after we fucked on Wednesday, all I wanted to do was write it down and relive it again through the diary. But I'm glad for it. Having this outlet has been very important to me, and that's become more and more apparent as we are nearing the end of your course. Soon I'll be stumbling out into the big wide acting world on my own. Vanessa has been trying to get me to take an Animal Theory class with her, but the thought of spending weeks on end pretending to be a cat or an orang-utan really doesn't thrill me! I have this feeling that I'm preparing to jump in at the deep end and see if I can swim . . .

I mean, I still have my moments of doubt, don't get me wrong. I am dreading the end of the classes – my entire week is just a preamble to you: to seeing you, to listening to you teach us – in your cantankerous way – this fantastic craft and the best ways to use it; the thrill of giving you my diary, of wondering what you have thought; the worry over whether my attraction to you is getting in the way of my getting the best from all of this. Or whether it is, in fact, making me a better actor . . . I think it is. I feel strong and free in ways I never did before I came to London, before I met you.

It's funny that we were doing the justification classes on Friday. It got me thinking about the position I find myself in now, with one more week of being guaranteed of seeing you. One more week of being justified in writing this diary and giving it to you. We're coming to the end of this little exercise . . . and, despite our physical connections, I don't know what my expectations can really be with you. I'm too much of a coward to question you about this to your face, I know. But there was something you said that really caught my attention when you gave back the diary after class on Friday . . .

I loved, first of all, that you apologized for not giving it back sooner – you had stopped by once or twice but I wasn't in and you wanted to give it back in person . . . I knew it wasn't just the diary you wanted to give me, from the glint in your eye as you said it. You told me you were impressed with my memory – I said it was pretty hard to forget. You leaned closer to me – there were only one or two other students milling around before class. You waited until you were sure they were looking in the other direction, and then you brushed your lips against mine. I sighed. Just that briefest of touches made my pussy tingle. And then you said the thing that has been playing on my mind. You pulled away, and then in a low, almost sad whisper, you said –

'I'm going to miss you, Toni. It's rare that I find a girl I can really trust.'

But before I could say anything in return, more students filed in and came up to you to chat and ask questions, oblivious to me and my tribulations. It's driving me wild, wanting to know what you meant by that. I got the feeling you were letting me in a little when we met Marguerite at the bar – that perhaps you were trusting me, letting me into your life, if only in a very roundabout way. But I didn't like something about the tone, the mysteriousness, and the finality of what you said. Then again, I know I shouldn't be surprised at not being able to understand you after all that has happened . . . I just don't want to be let down.

TUESDAY 17TH JANUARY

I came home this evening to be greeted by a newly coupled-up Vanessa. She pounced on me and couldn't wait to tell me all about their fantastic trip to Rome, the number of times they'd had sex and where, which of the locations was her favourite (the balcony – apparently the possibility of hurtling to certain death on to the cobbled stone road below only heightened all her sensations!). It was really good to have her back though, and to have someone to talk to. I was beginning to feel sorry for myself after so many days of not seeing you. I popped round to your house yesterday evening, but you seemed distracted and so when your phone rang, it seemed like the right time to excuse myself. You were friendly, but a little distant all of a sudden. I don't know what's wrong and I'm beginning to get a bit paranoid about it.

Still, I couldn't help but tell Vanessa about what had happened between us last week. I know it's a bit unethical to sleep with your teacher, but there's only one class left and I didn't think she would be too horrified – of course, it was quite the opposite. She was rapturous with glee as I told her about our night together. It comforted me, but also made me a little sad that things hadn't gone quite as I had wished in my heart of hearts. I know I'm being a little unrealistic, and I can't pretend that I didn't have some idea of what I might be getting into going down this more intimate path with you, but nevertheless, I am anxious to know once and for all where I stand.

But the main news of the evening lurked in Nessa's copy of *The Stage*. There, in an unassuming corner of the classified section, was a notice for open auditions for the premiere of Brad Goldberg's *Straight Through Sunday Blues*. The play was finally going ahead. All this work was going to pay off at last. It was what we had been building towards. Both of us were gripped with excitement. And something else took hold of me – an unshakable determination that I was going to perform the best audition I possibly could. This is what I had been waiting for . . . now was my chance. I'm going to use my newly kindled sexual awareness, all these tools you have taught me and, most of all, the massive frustrations you have driven me to, and now I am going to go out and get what I have wanted the most all along.

CHAPTER TEN

GIVEN CIRCUMSTANCES

This is it. I don't know what to say. I don't know how far you think you've come, or whether in fact you have learned anything at all from my meaningless ramblings each week, but for what it's worth, here we are at the end. Now the only thing left for you to do is roll all this shit up into a ball in your minds and keep it safe, and if you're lucky it'll get you through. Use these tools and then take the material you are working with and create a backbone that you can take and prop up the rest of your performance with. The circumstances that the author has provided for you – the time, the place, the feelings, the other people in the scenes. You need to be able to summarize in a handful of words exactly what the backbone of it all is. Then you will be on your way.

Because, you see, you're not on your own. You're being guided by the circumstances presented to you. You are working towards a very specific set of goals, and number one on that list is honesty. We as an audience have to believe in you. If we do . . . well, you're on your way.

MONDAY 23RD JANUARY
This feels strange. Knowing that this is the last time I'm going to write in here. Knowing that, despite our living so close to one another, there is the possibility

I may never see you again. Strange, but . . . somehow it feels right too. Complete, in a way. If nothing else, I know I will miss the classes, studying this great craft of ours, challenging myself on that kind of level every week. I'll miss watching you work, your gruff, cantankerous manner hiding a genuine love of acting, and of teaching us. You don't have to always put up that wall, you know – letting us see over it won't make us respect you any less. It certainly didn't stop me from respecting you.

But anyway, the last class of the course was very useful as it turns out. Going through the Goldberg play and breaking it down, looking at all the different elements and creating a blueprint from which to work was invaluable in what happened for me today . . . Before I started your classes, I had never really thought about how much of acting is purely cerebral. Thinking things through, breaking them down. Rolling them around in your mind. And in turn, how much of that can be applied to life – to love. And, most especially, to sex. Writing in here has been the most sexually freeing thing I have ever done, and although I know . . . what I know now about your intentions, it has had such an impact on my life, in ways that maybe you hadn't even intended. It hasn't only affected my acting, but everything I do, the way I approach things, the way I feel about my body, my sexuality and myself. And these things in turn have affected my acting in a more positive way than I could ever have imagined.

In class on Friday, sitting in huddled groups on the floor, highlighter pens and notebooks at the ready, going through the text and really analysing it, felt good. It was the first time I felt like a bona fide actress, preparing myself for the dramatic challenges ahead. It got me thinking about everything that has happened over the past few months. Considering the risks I have taken, the circumstances…

I sat down the day before class and read through everything I've written in here. It made me realize just how far I've come, literally and emotionally. Moving here was the best thing I have ever done. And even though it's been challenging, and you've been there through all this, guiding me, I know that if it wasn't for me taking that initial risk, making that ultimate decision to come here and pursue my dreams despite all the obvious misgivings, then I never would have arrived at the place I find myself in today. It's a very empowering feeling, and I am grateful to you for bringing out that analytical side in me.

But what happened after class last week . . . I thought I was prepared to confront anything, but of course, I should have expected that you would have one last trick up your sleeve. Before the class began you came over to me and asked if I could wait behind afterward. I knew we needed to talk things out, given that the whole situation between the two of us was still lingering in ambiguity. I had been preparing myself for a 'chat' about what might happen after the end of the course. And I had been dreading it, because I knew what the outcome would be. Or at least I thought I did. Turns out I was only partly right, I suppose.

I had to linger conspicuously when the class ended, for what felt like a lifetime. Several of the students were eager to let you know how grateful they were for your course, how much they admired you, and so forth. More than a few of them were clearly angling for you to help them with various auditions or help recommend them for other classes that were notoriously difficult to get into. You were gracious, and were clearly trying to avoid being too dismissive, but you kept glancing over to make sure I was still there waiting for you. Vanessa made a slightly reluctant but subtle retreat, although I could tell she was dying to know what he might say. I was at the point of bursting myself. Finally, the last of the students made their way to the door. I began to walk towards you from the back of the room, feeling as though I was watching a movie – a slow-motion zoom to a close-up of your face as I reached where you were standing and stood in front of you at last.

You seemed a little anxious, as though you weren't quite sure where to begin. You sighed and shuffled from foot to foot, brushing your hair off your forehead with an air of exasperation. It was quite endearing, but I couldn't tell whether it was just because of the awkwardness of the situation, or whether you were concerned about something else. Neither of us had spoken for a couple of minutes, but I felt I had to say something to break the silence. So I rummaged around in my bag and pulled out the diary. It felt unfinished, not having had a chance to write about the final class, get that feeling of completion. But I wasn't sure whether I would have another opportunity to give it to you, once and for all, so it seemed best to hand it over while I had the chance.

Trying to keep my tone light, I said, 'Well, here it is. The masterwork in all its glory . . .' I smiled a self-conscious smile.

You let out a small chuckle, but didn't take it. Instead, you slipped your hands into your pockets and said, 'No, you should keep it.'

I wanted to tell you that the greatest pleasure I derived from writing my diary was the very fact that your eyes would be skimming across every word, that it didn't work if you weren't on the other end. Every word in here is for you. But, despite your continuous pleas for honesty in our acting, somehow I felt that you weren't quite ready for any great face-to-face declarations of emotional connection. So I just stood there, not quite sure what to say next. But you spoke first.

'Toni, I need to talk to you . . . I mean, obviously, I'm talking to you. I need to tell you something. About all of this. About what we've been doing.'

My heart began to thump in my chest; I could feel my pulse throbbing in my temples. I tried my best to appear calm, but I couldn't will the next words to come out of your mouth fast enough. I had no idea what this new revelation was going to be, but from the furrowed brow and uncomfortable demeanour you were displaying, I had the distinct feeling it wasn't going to be anything good. You seemed to be struggling to find a way to phrase what it was you were going to say, and so we spent agonizing minutes looking at each other and looking away again, and every passing moment made my heart rise further and further into my throat. At last, you spoke again.

'Over these past few weeks, I have watched you really blossom. You've come a lot further than I could ever have imagined you would, and I don't mean that in a patronizing way. I knew you had a great deal of potential or I never would have asked you to . . . This has been one of the most confusing periods that I have ever been confronted with in my life. These things have always been so simple going in at the start, and I've found that, overall, they've been effective, but somehow you managed to take it to this level that I've never previously had to deal with. And it's had an impact on me that I never expected.'

I had no idea what you meant, and was getting more and more anxious and confused by the second. I think you could see the look on my face conveying my growing panic, and for some reason it made you smile, then grin broadly. It was infectious, and in spite of myself I felt the corners of my mouth begin to turn upward.

'Look, I apologize. I don't mean to be overdramatic.' The irony of your statement made us both chuckle again. And then you reached up and brushed aside a stray curl from my face, with this mixture of affection and something bordering on regret – it made my heart melt. You continued . . .

'I just don't want you to come out of this with a false sense of what had happened – good or bad. I just want to be . . . honest.' Your expression became serious again, and your eyes drilled into me, searchingly. You wanted to be absolutely certain it was all sinking in.

'When all this began, I asked you to show me your diary because I saw a potential in you that stood out amongst all of the others. It's something I have been doing for a while, since I started teaching the course. I'm always looking out for that person in the class who has something . . . special. And it's not always that I deliberately single out a woman per se, it's just that . . . that's the way it has been over the past few goes around on this little experiment.'

You paused, assessing my reaction. I tried not to betray anything but I couldn't disguise the perplexed look on my face. As you began to speak again, you placed a hand on my arm and your voice softened.

'I don't want you to think that this hasn't been an incredibly unique experience. It has. It's been . . . I always try to keep myself distanced. I want that person, the person I choose, to feel a sense of growth, but I try not to interfere on a personal level. The reason that I ask whomever it is that I single out to write the diary and let me read it is because I want them to have a heightened sense of self-awareness when they are writing. I want them to feel like they have to be more conscious of what they write because there will be another person on the receiving end of those words.

'I have found that people seem to use it as an outlet for all sorts of things, for feelings that may not ever have come out if they had just kept a diary for themselves. And, I admit, the nature of this has meant that some of these students have become rather emotionally attached to me. But I've never . . . I mean, like I say, I've tried to keep it impersonal . . .'

You seemed to lose your train of thought for a moment. I stood, open-mouthed and incredulous at everything you had just said. I felt a rising tide of anger begin to envelop me. Before you could begin again, I interrupted.

'You used me? I'm just one of many pathetic girls who have fallen prey to you, to your ridiculous experiment? How do you expect me to react to that? You've tried to keep it impersonal? What the hell do you mean by that? What, so all those mind games, all those challenges, the times we fucked? What was all of that? Strictly business, was it?'

I was shaking with anger and I could feel tears beginning to well up in my eyes, but I blinked them away furiously. You seemed taken aback at my tirade of questions, and didn't quite know where to start.

'Toni, I didn't want to upset you, I just had to get it out in the open. I never . . . I haven't ever told any of the others about this, but that's just it! With you . . . try as I could to get it to stop, you got under my skin. It was personal. What you wrote . . . the freedom you seemed to gain with every word . . . I couldn't resist you.'

That compliment, combined with the fact that you looked so genuinely hurt by my anger, meant that it began to subside, despite part of me wanting to storm off and never speak to you again. I asked you to continue.

'I'm sorry, Toni. I didn't mean for it to get so out of control. I just wanted to encourage you. To allow you to realize the true extent of your potential. But there was this other side to it, you were so sensual . . . I could never understand the way you seemed to be almost jealous of Vanessa, of Veronica . . . I mean, of course, they have an air about them that is obviously sexual, but with you, it was just so deliciously below the surface, and every time I would read one of your diary entries . . . You just broke me down piece by piece.

'And I'm not saying it was purely about that, but it just opened my eyes to you in a way that they have never been opened with the others I've asked to do this. You seemed to know how to get to me, and after a while I just had to give in.'

We stood in silence, your words still ringing in my ears. I think you may have thought that I wasn't planning to say anything at all as I stood there, looking at the ground with my arms folded in front of me. I needed a while to process what you had said to me, but as you began to put your notes away quietly and slip your jacket on, I had to say something. I couldn't let you just walk away.

'Marcus.' It felt strange to say your name out loud like that. You stopped, and looked at me.

'Marcus – wait. I just . . . this is just so much to take on board. But I do want you to know that I appreciate what you've done for me. And I appreciate you being honest with me, at last. This has been . . . well, you know this already, you've read it. But it's been one of the most important periods of my life. Coming here, not really knowing what I was getting myself into . . .

This was exactly what I needed. You've helped me become the woman, and the actress, that I wanted to be . . . and I'm proud of what I have achieved on both counts. So, thank you . . .'

And then, almost impulsively, I moved closer to you and slipped my arms around your waist underneath your jacket, holding you close to me one last time. I tilted my face towards you and pressed my lips to yours. It wasn't like the other times I had kissed you, though. It wasn't feverish or desperate. It was a beautiful, gentle kiss. We stayed locked together like that for a long time. Then you brought your hands up so they balanced softly against each of the round halves of my bottom. You pulled your face away from mine for a moment with a sly, sexy grin playing across your features. Then you kissed me again, the passion once again sparking electricity between your lips and mine. We kissed one another deeply, and I could feel you beginning to get hard against my hip through our clothes. I began to chuckle and pulled away, smiling. Much as I wanted to, I knew that it was time for me to go. You smiled back at me, knowingly.

I moved away and walked towards the door. Just before I left, I stopped and turned around. You were watching me go with that mysterious, sexy look glinting in your eye. I started to say something else, but stopped myself, and instead just told you –

'I'm going to miss you, Marcus.'

And I was gone.

I wanted to let you know that I had gone to the audition for the Goldberg play, and that I had used everything that I had learned over these past few weeks, gathered up all of my energy, and completely nailed my audition.

They short-listed me for a call-back, this afternoon. And I just found out that I got it. I'm going to play Angelique. I decided to finish off my diary entries and come round and drop this off at your house. But when I got home just now, still buzzing from them letting me know I had got the part, I found a note lying on my mat. It's from you. And it just says:

'I knew you could do it.'

But what surprises me the most is not just that you believed in me, but that I truly believed in myself.